YO-AET-451

"We need to get as far away as we can before they come back."

Gwen straightened her shoulders. "Then let's not waste any time."

He couldn't possibly have gotten any luckier in a partner, Rafe thought.

Rafe wasn't much for introspection. He compartmentalized, too, as most people in his line of work did. He thought of himself as a compassionate man; he'd give his life for that of an innocent, no hesitation. But day to day...he calculated in terms of how events and people would help or hinder him on the job.

That's what he'd just done.

Gwen Allen was a gutsy woman who improved his chances of escaping this disaster and making it to court to bring down a lot of bad guys.

But what would the fallout be for her—assuming both of them in fact survived? Keeping her alive had been a high priority for him, but was that enough?

CRASH LANDING

USA TODAY Bestselling Author

JANICE KAY JOHNSON

If you purchased this book without a cover you should be aware
that this book is stolen property. It was reported as "unsold and
destroyed" to the publisher, and neither the author nor the
publisher has received any payment for this "stripped book."

For Pat aka Alexis Morgan,
an amazing friend and plotting partner

Recycling programs
for this product may
not exist in your area.

ISBN-13: 978-1-335-59083-1

Crash Landing

Copyright © 2024 by Janice Kay Johnson

All rights reserved. No part of this book may be used or reproduced in
any manner whatsoever without written permission except in the case of
brief quotations embodied in critical articles and reviews.

This is a work of fiction. Names, characters, places and incidents
are either the product of the author's imagination or are used fictitiously.
Any resemblance to actual persons, living or dead, businesses, companies,
events or locales is entirely coincidental.

For questions and comments about the quality of this book, please contact us
at CustomerService@Harlequin.com.

TM and ® are trademarks of Harlequin Enterprises ULC.

Harlequin Enterprises ULC
22 Adelaide St. West, 41st Floor
Toronto, Ontario M5H 4E3, Canada
www.Harlequin.com

Printed in U.S.A.

An author of more than ninety books for children and adults with more than seventy-five for Harlequin, **Janice Kay Johnson** writes about love and family and pens books of gripping romantic suspense. A *USA TODAY* bestselling author and an eight-time finalist for the Romance Writers of America RITA® Award, she won a RITA® Award in 2008. A former librarian, Janice raised two daughters in a small town north of Seattle, Washington.

Books by Janice Kay Johnson

Harlequin Intrigue

Hide the Child
Trusting the Sheriff
Within Range
Brace for Impact
The Hunting Season
The Last Resort
Cold Case Flashbacks
Dead in the Water
Mustang Creek Manhunt
Crime Scene Connection
High Mountain Terror
The Sheriff's to Protect
Crash Landing

Visit the Author Profile page at Harlequin.com.

CAST OF CHARACTERS

Gwen Allen—A paramedic with a helicopter rescue service, Gwen isn't supposed to be on the flight that goes so terribly wrong. But how much worse would it all have been if she had listened to her doubts and refused to board?

Rafe Salazar—A DEA agent who has been undercover with a drug cartel for over a year, Rafe is badly wounded when the location of his safe house is betrayed. Snatched out of the hospital, he might survive only thanks to the paramedic he wants to trust.

Bruce Kimball—Also a DEA agent, Kimball has begun to have second thoughts about his future. One big payoff could change everything.

Bill Thomson—A former military helicopter pilot, Bill is a new hire with the rescue service. He doesn't quite understand all the rules yet, or see why making a small exception could lead to deadly consequences.

Ron Zabrowsky—Salazar's supervisor in the DEA is stunned by what almost has to be an internal betrayal, and then having his injured agent—whose testimony is critical to bring down a drug trafficking organization—simply disappear off the face of the earth.

Chapter One

Gwen Allen inhaled the powerful smell of hot jet fuel as she walked across the tarmac toward one of the two helicopters parked near the long, low building that served as the base for EMS Flight, the helicopter rescue service she worked for. Her small rolling suitcase bumped along with her, and her enormous tote bag weighed heavily on her shoulder.

Her home base with EMS Flight was just outside Seattle, but she'd spent a week visiting a good friend from college in Yakima, Washington, on the dry side of the Cascade mountains. The very dry side. Heat radiated off the paved surface and it felt as if it were baking any exposed skin to leather. Within her fire-retardant Nomex suit, she was even hotter. She'd enjoyed a few days of sunshine—Seattle was having an unusually cool July—but she wouldn't want to live and work in this climate. Imagine how blistering August and September would be! Still, she was glad she'd been able to borrow the suit and a helmet from the locker of a nurse who was taking maternity leave.

Eyes on the two Bell helicopters painted with the familiar red and green stripes against an overall white, Gwen felt like skipping. A week ago, she'd gotten lucky enough to hitch a ride over with a coworker driving to Spokane, almost to the Idaho border, but she'd planned to either buy an airline ticket or hop a Greyhound bus for her return. Wonder of wonders, a guy in base dispatch had called yesterday to let her know they were transferring a helicopter to her base on a temporary basis to replace one that would be out for much-needed maintenance. Someone had mentioned she was in Yakima and planning to travel back at about the right time. Did she want a ride? She'd be alone with the pilot, no patient to monitor.

Of course, she could have afforded to pay for the trip home, but this way, she could tuck a few more dollars into her dream fund.

Only, to her puzzlement, an ambulance had just pulled up behind the Bell 419 helicopter she thought was supposed to be her ride, and as she watched, EMTs from the ambulance unloaded a patient packaged on a backboard and transferred him or her to the helicopter.

Nobody at all stood by the second helicopter.

Probably that pilot had already done his pre-flight and retreated back into the building, and she was heading for the wrong one.

She took out her phone to check the time. They were supposed to lift off five minutes from now.

She'd been a paramedic with EMS Flight for two years now after working on an ambulance and in the emergency department at Swedish Hospital in Seattle. She'd studied hard for the certifications required. She loved her job and the adrenaline boost with every rescue. The thing was, among her coworkers, she liked order and the certainty she could absolutely rely on them.

If that was her helicopter, the pilot had probably taken a last-minute restroom run, something she'd just done, too. In prep for the flight to Seattle, she'd restricted her fluid intake, too. She was fussing. Not like they were in any hurry.

The patient was now on board the helicopter right in front of her, the door closed. The rotors weren't turning yet, so she presumed the man in the Nomex suit sewn with the company patch was the pilot. The other guy wore chinos and a denim shirt open over a T-shirt. Who was *he*? Friend or family of the patient?

She'd almost reached them when they noticed her. The second guy moved fast to intercept her. His body language was weirdly aggressive enough that she had the sense he was blocking her.

"What are you doing out here?" he demanded.

"Is this the helicopter going to Seattle?"

"Who are you?" he asked impatiently.

By most women's standards, he was handsome. Sandy brown hair, square jaw, tall, nice shoulders. Gwen did not like the cold, verging-on-hostile way he was eyeing her.

"A paramedic with EMS Flight," she said shortly. She tapped the logo patch on her shoulder that said EMS followed by a bird in flight. "Who are *you*?"

Instead of answering, he turned just enough to wave the pilot over. "Bill?"

This man, somewhere around forty years old, was friendly looking, thin, with military-short hair, which didn't surprise her. Many of the pilots were ex-military. Knowing the training and experience they brought with them inspired a level of trust in the nurses, EMTs and paramedics who relied on their expertise.

She held out her hand. "Gwen Allen, a paramedic with EMS Flight, but out of Seattle."

"Oh, ah. We were told the nurse scheduled to fly with us couldn't make it. We were just talking about what to do."

"You're the pilot?"

"Yes. Sorry. Bill Thomson."

"Then…this isn't the helicopter being trans-ferred to Seattle?"

"Yeah, it is," he said readily. "That's our end goal, but we, uh, kind of got hijacked." He nod-ded toward Mr. Unpleasant. "Law enforcement. I'm new with EMS Flight, but I'm told we try to help out whenever any LEA asks for help."

That was true, but law enforcement agencies typically called when they had a severely in-jured victim that needed quick transport with expert care. They didn't "hijack" a flight.

"So," she said, still trying to understand, "you don't have a nurse or paramedic, but you do have a patient?"

"That's right."

"We don't need a medical attendant," Mr. Unfriendly said. "We're transporting a man who had surgery some hours ago. He's stable. I'm assured there's no reason to expect a prob-lem. I'm an agent with the Drug Enforcement Administration, and we want him moved to Se-attle, get him checked out so he can be trans-ferred to where he belongs."

The distaste and heightened hostility in his voice made it seem as if this patient was, if not dangerous, someone whose crimes were con-temptible. A recent arrest, presumably.

Bill's phone rang, then hers. She glanced at

the number. Dispatch. She let the call go to voice mail, but saw that Bill had half turned away and was talking on his phone, his gaze staying on her. He gave her a nod.

She concentrated on the circumstances. This wouldn't be the first time the patient her team had rushed to pick up was someone who'd be placed under arrest—if he survived grave wounds. She'd given her all to save the life of many a street criminal.

"What kind of surgery?" she asked.

"He took two bullets."

She waited. No more information was apparently forthcoming.

"If I'm going to handle his or her care on this flight, I'll need to know more."

"His. But I told you. We don't—"

"You do," she interrupted, making sure there was no give in her voice. "The company does not allow a helicopter carrying a patient to take off without trained medical personnel on board." She shifted her gaze, raising her eyebrows. Fortunately, Bill had ended his call. "Isn't that right, Bill?"

"That's what I was just telling Agent Kimball," he agreed with a sidelong glance at his companion. "That was dispatch on the phone," he added. "I've only been with the company a month, though, and have never run into a situation like this. Er, Agent Kimball plans to fly with us."

"Salazar needs to remain under supervision by a law enforcement agent," Kimball said. "If he breaks free, you couldn't handle him."

"Okay," she said. "Where are you taking him?"

"The university hospital in Seattle."

The teaching hospital in Seattle was definitely where you wanted to go if you had any unusual problems. But if this guy had come out of surgery in good enough shape that his surgeon had anticipated no problems and okayed a long and uncomfortable helicopter flight, why send him there?

For someone who liked to be prepared, she had a lot of qualms: Was there even a trauma bag on board? If so, who had packed it? Before they lifted off from the ground, she could hustle to do some of her preflight checks, but there were half a dozen tasks she always completed at the start of her shift so there were no later surprises. She started running through potential issues in her mind. Had the levels of oxygen in the tanks been checked? Unexpectedly running out *was* a major crisis. Plugs and inverter functioning? Were they stocked on batteries for handheld devices? This would be an unusually long flight. EKG patches…

She cut herself off. The pilot had seen the patient, so she wasn't relying a hundred percent on Agent Kimball saying the guy was in peachy keen condition. The EMTs on the ambulance must not have been concerned, or they'd have waited to do an in-person handover.

And, hey, she'd not only get a free ride home, the company would now have to pay her for her services. That made her feel a little more cheerful. No reason to think there'd be any issues.

Famous last words, a voice whispered in her head. She ignored it.

"Fine," she said. "Then let's get on our way."

There was a short silence that felt…odd. Gwen didn't know how to read it. Neither man looked at each other, yet she had the weird sense that they were conferring, anyway. Maybe she *didn't* want to get on this helicopter, especially without having done her own preflight check.

Except…there was a patient who needed her. Besides, working with people who were new hires or pains in the butt wasn't out of the ordinary, and cops she dealt with at accident or crisis sites were given to being dictatorial with the medical team, wanting to give orders when that was no longer their place. The fact that she found DEA agent Kimball annoying was no reason to refuse to do her job *and* get a free— no, paid!—ride home.

"Works for me." Bill sounded agreeable, and

his wink at her was reassuring, hinting that he, too, found Kimball difficult.

"Fine," Kimball grumbled. "What's one more?"

Normally, if she were heading a team, she'd ride up front next to the pilot, in part to watch for potential hazards in the air and at a landing site. Of course, in that case, there would also be a nurse or EMT at the side of the patient.

Even as they walked the short distance to board the helicopter, she made up her mind: she was staying in back with the man who definitely needed monitoring and might need intercession. Agent Kimball could sit up front, where she mostly wouldn't be able to see a face that radiated impatience and irritation as much as the vast paved tarmac did heat.

Maybe, it occurred to her, he'd been relegated to what he considered to be scut work and resented it. After all, how challenging was accompanying a semiconscious, restrained man? She could give him a break.

RAFE HAD NO idea what was happening to him. He had a vague notion that he was in recovery at the hospital, except for some reason, he'd been trussed up like a Christmas tree ready to be stuffed in the rear hatch of a car to be sure branches weren't broken.

He opened his eyes and felt a surge of panic.

Why couldn't he see anything? He hadn't been blinded, had he? He tried to lift a hand to his face, but a tight restraint kept him from raising his arm. A minute ago, whatever he was lying on had tilted upright enough that he'd tried to grab for purchase, but then it leveled off.

The reason he should be—would have sworn he *was*—in the hospital flashed in jerky movements as if filmed with a handheld camera that often wasn't pointing the way it should be.

Knock on the front door; Eaton muting the TV and going to the door to look through the peephole. Stanton was there, too. Rafe saw him stiffen and unsnap his holster. They weren't expecting anyone. But Eaton immediately relaxed and unlocked and then started to open the door.

"Hey." Clearly, he knew the visitor. "What are you doing here?"

A burst of gunfire. Stanton yelling, "Run," as bullets sprayed the living room. Rafe leaped to his feet, bounced off the wall in the hall and spun into a bedroom. Smashed a chair through the window and dove out, a lilac bush scratching him as he fell. One arm useless. He rolled, seeing a man framed by the window he'd just thrown himself out of. More gunfire. Bullets struck his torso, and his body repeatedly jerked. Nothing hurt yet, but it would. Why had

*he been so complacent, he wasn't carrying this
evening? Were his bodyguards down? Must be.*

*Voices raised, sirens. He couldn't see anyone
through the jagged-edged windowpane now.
Couldn't help closing his eyes.*

It was all vivid but chaotic.

Didn't help him understand where he was
now or why.

Then everything around him began to vibrate.

THE TWO MEN seemed to be engaged in a low-
voiced intense conversation from the minute
they took their seats in front. But Bill did turn
his attention to business because the engines
fired up.

After stowing her suitcase out of the way,
Gwen scanned the cabin as she hurried through
some of what should have been preflight checks,
and her gaze caught on the surprising sight of
what appeared to be a fully loaded backpack
with a sleeping bag tied on. She tugged to be
sure it was adequately wedged in so it wouldn't
become a missile if the flight turned out to be
turbulent. *Is it Bill's?* she wondered idly, then
put it out of her mind.

She leaned over the patient to make a quick
evaluation of his condition before she flipped
through his chart. To look at his dressings, she'd

have to pull back blankets, but that meant first undoing straps that kept him immobilized. That could wait. He wasn't on oxygen, but she considered putting him on it. Better to be preventative than to react to trouble. What surprised her was that thick foam plugs had been inserted in his ears, and a black mask covered his eyes. She hoped somebody had explained what they were doing before depriving him of two major senses. There were reasons why it was sometimes a good idea, but... He might freak if he'd still been in a hazy postanesthetic state and now surfaced to find himself blind and deaf.

She glanced at the manila envelope with a sticker on the front identifying him as one Rafael Salazar. Hair very dark, maybe black, disheveled and spiky from whatever he'd been through. Skin darker than hers that stretched over sharp cheekbones. Dark stubble on a strong jaw. Probably a good-looking guy. It was hard to be sure under the circumstances and didn't matter, anyway.

Besides...criminal, she reminded herself, even as instinct had her smoothing his hair back from his forehead.

She made herself take her own seat and belted herself in. Borrowed helmet—check. Somewhere in her bag were her own earplugs, but she didn't always wear them, and that could wait.

Normally, part of her job was handling four radio frequencies, although today not quite as many would be required. The pilot had several, too. Right now, she had to wait for the intercom to come on to talk to him.

"Gwen?" Bill's voice came in her ears. "Barring any problem, I'll need you to let me handle radio communications once we've lifted off. Agent Kimball is insistent that we stay off the air as much as possible. The agency would just as soon no one knows who we're transporting or where he's being taken. Or even that we have a federal agent on board."

Her forehead crinkled. It wasn't as if she'd have chatted on the radio about her patient, and they were still required to connect with local controllers along the way in part to make sure there were no midair collisions. This flight had been scheduled to be routine. Why would anyone, hearing them confirm altitude, direction or ETA—destination, for that matter—suspect for a moment that they carried a federal agent and his prisoner? Did Agent Kimball think they'd be shot out of the sky if the wrong people learned who was aboard?

Ridiculous.

As for the radio, a former military pilot would probably be accustomed to handling complex communications, or he wouldn't sound so casual about it.

Still, the unusual request ratcheted up Gwen's unease. Company policy was that if any member of the team felt strongly that the flight wouldn't be safe—usually because of expected severe weather—and refused to go, the mission was canceled, and the helicopter stayed grounded. Period. In these circumstances, Gwen could demand an okay from someone higher up the chain of authority.

Feeling vaguely unsettled didn't justify that step, she decided. Honestly, if Agent Kimball had been friendly and more open with her, she wouldn't be as uneasy as she was.

"Sure, Bill," she said. "Let me know if you need me to jump on."

"Will do." He still sounded cheerful. The pilots she knew best were happiest in the air or maneuvering to land at a tricky site.

She double-checked her seat belt and the patient's restraints, then felt the helicopter lift off. She remembered her terror on her first flights when she looked at the radio console, with a zillion buttons and switches. Like most newbies, she'd made mistakes. Today...she could switch most of them off. Why listen if she was supposed to keep her mouth shut?

Over the noise of the engines, she couldn't

even hear Bill confirm departure with base dispatch, but she could see him at an oblique angle. He was talking into his mic, seeming relaxed.

As the ground below them receded, she felt some of her usual excitement. No, they weren't racing to the scene of an auto accident where cops were even now employing the Jaws of Life to pry someone out of a dangerously compressed space, or aiming to pick up a mountain climber who'd fallen and suffered unknown injuries, or collecting a kid who'd been shot while playing with a gun.

Her gaze rested again on the man who lay within hand's reach—the man who *had* been shot twice. By the cops trying to arrest him? Clearly, she was never going to know.

Oxygen? she asked herself again. It wouldn't hurt anything, and even if it wasn't otherwise needed, it combated nausea and motion sickness.

Studying him, she was troubled to see movement, as if he were fighting against the restraints. No matter what, he had to remain secured in case of unexpected turbulence, but she could talk to him.

She could see part of the back of Kimball's head and one ear, but he couldn't get a good look at what she was doing. So she leaned forward, eased the foam plug from the patient's ear and spoke as close to it as possible. As it was, she had to raise her voice to have any chance of being heard.

"How are you doing? I'm Gwen, taking care of you during a helicopter ride, in case you wondered why your whole body is vibrating."

His head turned, just the slightest amount. Her lips brushed his ear.

She stole another look at Kimball, then pushed the mask up to Rafael Salazar's forehead. His eyes opened briefly. He squeezed them shut, then opened them again and stared blankly upward. Finally, he managed to focus on her face.

Those eyes were a rich brown—*dark chocolate*, she thought. He hadn't regained complete clarity postsurgery but was close to it.

He stared for so long that she repeated her introduction and explanation of where they were. "Do you understand?" she asked.

He swallowed, worked his mouth and finally spoke a single word. "Yes." Pause. "Where?"

She spoke slowly, and only after another glance to be sure Kimball couldn't see her or, presumably, hear her, given the noise made by the engines. "I understand we're transporting you to Harborview Hospital in Seattle to make sure the surgery you underwent in Yakima is all you need."

"Surgery?"

"I'm told you were shot twice. Do you remember?"

"Yeah." Another swallow. "Yes."

"Good." She smiled instead of apologizing for her choice of words. Unlikely *he* thought being shot twice was good. "Let me know if you become nauseated, hurt too much, feel anything unexpected. Okay?"

"Gwen?" A voice came through her earpieces. Bill, she realized.

"Yes?"

"Everything okay?" he asked.

"Yep."

"Agent Kimball would prefer you don't make any attempt to communicate with the patient. He says Salazar is a dangerous man."

"Mr. Salazar seemed distressed, so I took out an earplug long enough to explain where he is and reassure him. That seemed to help."

The second voice didn't surprise her. "Unless he has a medical crisis, I'm asking you to keep your distance."

She felt steam building up. That was an order, not a request.

"Whatever you want to think, I don't work for you, Agent Kimball. The patient is in my charge until I hand him off to another medical professional."

She cut off his sputtering, at least temporarily, and met Salazar's eyes again. Something had changed. That gaze was sharp and alarmed, if she was reading it right. What had she said?

She opened her mouth…and he gave his head the tiniest shake, all the restraints permitted. But she understood: he didn't want her to continue challenging Kimball or to ask what might be the wrong questions.

Chapter Two

Had he heard her right? Agent *Kimball*? Rafe's brain tried to grind itself into motion despite the rust clogging it. What would Kimball be doing here? Rafe barely knew the man and didn't much like him. Unless he'd been transferred recently, he belonged in Chicago.

Must have heard this woman wrong, Rafe decided. Gwen… Allen? Something like that. She was taking care of him. Nurse? She didn't wear scrubs. Instead, her jumpsuit looked like what a navy pilot might wear. Rafe guessed it was made out of fire-retardant fabric, which made sense if they really were in a helicopter. Now that he could exam his surroundings, albeit in a limited way, he decided that's exactly where he was. A radio console with a forest of lights, switches and what have you, barely visible out of the corner of his eye, and a window taller than it was wide that let him see bright blue sky.

He'd thought the haze in his head was clearing, but if so, it was being replaced by a different kind of confusion. At the hospital, Zabrowsky's face had hovered over his for a few minutes. Rafe's supervising special agent must have been allowed into recovery in lieu of a next of kin. Rafe thought he'd mumbled a few questions that weren't answered, but he was quite sure nothing was said about shipping him across the state.

Was he more seriously wounded than the nurse in recovery had said? Possible, but where was Zabrowsky? How was a federal agent who should be in Chicago involved in the latest mess?

Which had started because Eaton had known whoever knocked on that door. The same someone who'd burst in firing a semiautomatic weapon, who'd chased Rafe into the bedroom and tried to gun him down. Unless the person who'd come by had been followed and had also been a victim?

None of this made sense. Rafe would give a lot to have been clearer in his head when Zabrowsky came to talk to him.

He studied the woman who was presumably a nurse or EMT. She appeared to be inspecting him with equal interest.

Her smooth hair, the color of maple syrup, was pulled back from her face and disappeared under a flight helmet. Eyes the rare gray of a dove's feathers, not so much penetrating as gentle. Fine-boned hands, slender build. He guessed tall but couldn't be sure. Her face drew him.

Would *she* answer any of his questions? He decided to try.

"Do you know how badly I'm hurt?"

Given the racket in here, she was probably lip-reading. She answered by bending again so that her mouth tickled his ear.

"Two gunshot wounds. If you'll wait a minute, I can read your chart."

"Yes."

He pondered her some more as she removed paperwork from a manila envelope and concentrated on every page. She didn't wear much if any makeup, he decided, although that might be the case only on the job. If she was a nurse, she might have to deal with squirting blood and the like, good reason not to bother with foundation or mascara. She didn't need it.

She shifted a little, setting aside a page, and he saw the patch on the upper arm of her Nomex suit. The letters EMS were part of a bird in flight. He guessed they were a rescue organization, the kind that plucked wounded or sick people from remote or difficult positions when ground transportation to a hospital would be too slow. He'd...encountered people from other such organizations before. Made him think of military medics. Same skill set, same personality type.

At last she raised her head, appeared to sneak a peek toward the front of the helicopter then leaned toward him.

"You took a bullet to your upper arm. That one will require physical therapy and conceivably additional surgery, because of the complexity of the rotator cuff where muscles and nerves are bundled together."

He tried for a nod but failed because his head, along with the rest of his body, was strapped down.

"Second bullet struck your thigh but missed the bone. You lost a lot of blood, though. You also have a cracked sternum and two broken ribs. I can't tell how those injuries came to be."

He could have enlightened her but chose not to. He might have been careless enough to leave his weapon in his bedroom, but he'd routinely worn a Kevlar vest, however relaxed he and his guards had become after over a month in the small ranch house in a working-class neighborhood in Yakima. Sounded like he'd be dead if he hadn't bothered with the vest.

He didn't remember noticing whether Eaton and Stanton had worn theirs. The air-conditioning only partially combated the summer heat, meaning vests weren't comfortable.

Why Yakima? Rafe wondered for probably the hundredth time. He'd barely heard of the town before getting deposited there. It had been settled on a river that joined the broad Columbia River not far downstream. These days, it was wine country, from what he understood, irrigated vineyards having supplanted other kinds of agriculture in the surrounding landscape. Wine grapes thrived in the hot, dry climate. That was the sum total of his knowledge of the town where he'd been prepared to stay for up to a year.

Gwen had flipped a couple more pages and now looked perturbed. Again, she leaned forward. "It sounds like you came through surgery with flying colors. Not sure what kind of follow-up they expect for you at Harborview, but it's a top-notch hospital, so you could have a worse destination."

Rafe only caught parts of what she said, given the engine noise. She seemed to be talking partly to herself, her puzzlement apparent.

He was becoming more aware of how much he hurt. Shouldn't he be in a hospital bed with a handy button within reach that he could push to boost the level of painkiller?

A memory niggled at him. He'd dated an ER

nurse, Nina Caldero, who said she'd worked helicopter rescue in Washington State for a few years. He thought this was the outfit she'd mentioned, which meant EMS Flight was reputable. A sense of wrongness still had Rafe's skin prickling, but he couldn't imagine Gwen or a pilot with the company cooperating in anything nefarious.

Maybe because he'd been on edge for so long—over a year now—it had become second nature to expect trouble. Literally tied down, there wasn't a damn thing he could do about it if his twitchy feeling was on target and everything was about to blow up in his face. Again. He might as well give in. The vibration and racket penetrating even the earplugs made his eyelids heavy. Maybe this would all make more sense if he slept for an hour or so.

Gwen must have thought the same or believed he'd already fallen asleep because he felt her touch as she replaced the plug in his ear. He was grateful she didn't cover his eyes again.

WATCHING THE MAN who slept beside her, Gwen began to feel a little drowsy herself. Flights weren't usually anywhere near this long. From takeoff, she'd have normally been mentally running over what equipment she'd need when they landed, what she could expect. Everyone on board would share the tension; they had a job to do, and it could go sideways in a heartbeat.

Today, she could have kicked back and admired the view from the window if it weren't for Rafael Salazar and his guard. She had a feeling Kimball wouldn't like knowing she'd talked to Salazar and began speculating even harder about why he was being taken to the hospital in Seattle. She felt sure the surgeons who'd operated on him in Yakima were competent.

She pulled a book from her tote and read for a while but found it hard to concentrate given that she also glanced up often to check on her patient. During one of those checks, some extra sense made her look out the window. Wisps of white appeared—and behind them was a sight any Washingtonian would know instantly: Mount Rainier, an active volcano that was the highest mountain in the lower forty-eight states. Black rock and glaciers forming a steep slope that plunged into the dark green of northwestern forests felt almost close enough to touch.

In other words, terrifyingly close.

Gwen snapped shut a mouth that had dropped open. As huge as the mountain was, she'd have expected a distant view of it as they crossed the

Cascade Range toward Seattle. There was no reason whatsoever they should be this close.

She used the mic to talk to Bill.

"Did you get lost?"

He chuckled. "No, Kimball wanted to see the mountain, and I didn't see any harm. We're not that far off course. Heck of a view, isn't it?"

"I'd like it better if it weren't for the clouds."

Whiteout could be a problem at higher elevations of a mountain that was over fourteen thousand feet and rose almost from sea level, unlike the Rocky Mountains. It seemed to Gwen that Bill was flirting with trouble. Micro weather events were the norm here. The National Park Service had their own resources for rescues on the mountain, including the giant Chinook helicopters from the army base, Fort Lewis, that could fly as high as the summit, which meant EMS Flight had never had reason to be in the vicinity.

Did Bill have any experience with the conditions he might meet here?

It's July, she reminded herself. Not exactly summer in the park, as it was elsewhere; snow would still be covering some trails, flowers just appearing in the meadows. She'd hiked one stretch of the Wonderland Trail that circled Mount Rainier. Eventually, she hoped to complete all of it, albeit one section at a time.

The engines sounded steady. She kept watching out the window, seeing less and less mountain, more and more clouds.

The helicopter gave an odd shudder.

Bill's voice in her ears. "Just a gust. I'm dropping in elevation."

Gwen had lost any hint of drowsiness. She sat tensely, expecting...she didn't know. The other shoe to drop in a day that was already peculiar.

"The fire light has come on," Bill suddenly snapped, a new sharpness in his voice.

She'd done the associated drills a hundred times. Her role right now was to look outside for smoke and identify where it was coming from. She all but did contortions to try to see where the trouble was, but the cloud cover had deepened, making it harder to pick out darker smoke.

"Nothing," she said. "Nothing."

"Damn it." Yes, there was mild tension in the pilot's voice, but mostly he sounded calm. A helicopter pilot with the experience he must have had to be hired by EMS Flight would remain calm and employ his every skill to, at worst, land the bird safely. "Going down," he added, confirming her suspicion. "Looking for a clear LZ."

LZ was the landing zone. Usually they'd be worrying about power wires, traffic and the competency of whatever firefighter, cop or ambulance crew had deemed a particular spot safe. Here, it would be too-steep slopes, enormous trees, tumbled boulders and lakes. Gwen wished intensely that she'd taken the seat beside Bill, where she could be of real help. That was a big part of her role, watching for unexpected trouble. What were the odds a DEA agent knew what a helicopter could handle and what would send it into a cataclysmic crash?

Instinctively, she tested the patient's restraints, then her own belt. She at least wore a helmet and a fire-retardant jumpsuit; Salazar was unlikely to have anything but scrubs on beneath the blankets that wrapped him. At least scrubs were cotton, better than fabrics that could melt into the skin.

If there was a fire, none of them were likely to survive. Even emergency medical helicopters staffed by experienced teams occasionally went down. Weather, rugged terrain, mechanical failure or a pilot's mistake could contribute. Right now, she couldn't see anything out the window except the lowering cloud cover, and the rocks and ice too close to her window.

The tail of the helicopter with the smaller rotor whipped subtly side to side.

The unusual movement had awakened the patient, whose dark eyes looked past her to a window, then fixed on her face. She sat close enough to him to remove both earplugs.

"Problem?"

"We should be fine," she shouted into his ear, "but we may have to set down. A warning light came on."

Still meeting Salazar's gaze, she sat back. "Bill?"

"We're dropping below the clouds. I think I see a potential LZ. Pretty lake. We can go fishing while we're here."

She could match his insouciance. "Just what I'd like to do today."

She heard an odd noise—somehow choked. Bill? *Please don't let him be having a heart attack, or—*

Abruptly, there was a hard thud after which they rocked, and suddenly she had the sense they were zigzagging. She automatically checked to be sure the oxygen was turned off, but of course it hadn't been on in the first place. Her patient didn't need it.

Bill had to be struggling to maintain control. What had really gone wrong? She wanted to talk to him but knew better than to distract him. Gwen focused on the view; she could see a glint of water, trees, a rocky buttress. No ideal place to set down.

And then they spun around entirely. Her fingers dug into the seat, as if she could hold herself in place. There was yelling, a screech of metal, and she knew they were down, bumping over rough ground. Her body was snapped forward, then back, and she knew vaguely that the top of the helicopter had been sheared off.

They came to a complete stop. The radio must have been damaged, because for a moment, the silence was absolute.

HER HANDS SHOOK as she unsnapped her seat belt and yelled to the front, "Bill? Kimball? Are you hurt?"

"I'm okay," the agent called back. "Pilot's unconscious."

"Get back here and help me unload the patient."

"What?" He must have unfastened his belt, too, because he'd twisted enough to look at her. "Why?"

"Fire. Jet fuel is incredibly volatile."

He let loose with some obscenities but, because the helicopter had become a convertible, was able to stand and step between seats. "We should get Bill first."

"No. Patient first. That's our protocol. He's completely helpless."

"You want *me* to help *him* first."

In the close quarters, she elbowed him out of

the way so she could free the backboard. "Yes! Let's move. Get him to a distance."

"I don't see any fire."

"I smell fuel. Try not to do anything that might incite a spark."

He went still for a moment, then his body language abruptly took on the urgency that she shared. Within moments, they'd heaved the backboard with a large man out an unapproved and usually nonexistent way. Once they were on the ground, she broke into a trot despite the weight she bore, and he did the same. Gwen didn't let herself stop until they were a good hundred yards from a helicopter that might blow sky high at any time. She was actually grateful for Kimball's strength, until he dropped his end without bothering to bend all the way. The sudden descent even to soft loam had to be painful for an already injured man.

Gwen finally turned to look at what had been a shiny, beautifully maintained helicopter and couldn't hold back a gasp.

The rotors at the rear were half drilled into the soil, half deep in a gash cut in a huge old tree. The main rotors were…gone. The cabin consisted of shards of metal that still formed a cup shape.

Kimball swore again beside her, sounding as shocked as she was.

She started at a trot back for the helicopter, calling urgently over her shoulder, "I'll grab what supplies I can. You wouldn't know what to get. Check on Bill. If he's alive, we'll have to pull him out even if we risk damaging his neck and spine."

If they had time, the chopper carried another backboard and a C-collar.

Time was something she was very afraid they didn't have.

Kimball looked reluctant, and she didn't blame him, but he was running beside her.

She lost sight of him when she clambered back inside the broken helicopter. The smell was almost overpowering, but she still didn't see any flicker of flame.

Hurry, she thought. Trauma bag first, her own tote that held some snack bars and other useful bits. Suitcase...no, the backpack. It had fallen and was wedged into an awkward spot, but the sleeping bag was something they might need if rescue didn't come quickly. Had Bill gotten off an emergency call?

Hurry.

Drugs. Only by long habit did she find her keys quickly and was able to fumble open the cabinet and narc box for pain relievers and syringes. Thank God EMS didn't require two people and two keys to get this open. Small bottles and more plastic syringes fell to her feet. She stuffed what was in her hand into the trauma bag. They had to get out of here... Her eye fell on a white plastic bag that was the kind the hospital used for a patient's personal effects. Salazar would need more clothing if they were here long.

There was nothing soft in the bag. Alarmingly, her fingers recognized the shape of a handgun. How could that be if he had been arrested?

She looped the strings over her arm, hefted the pack over her back and clambered back out, careful of the jagged metal. Not a good time to cut her own flesh open.

The moment her feet were on the ground, she broke into a run. She felt as if she were moving through sludge and bent under more pounds than she could possibly be carrying. Was she breathing in a whiff of smoke? Oh, God—hurry, hurry.

Kimball was already beside Salazar. Her first thought was to be mad. He could have tried to help her. But then her heart sank. He'd have called for her, surely, if Bill was alive but unconscious.

She fell to her knees beside the two men.

"Bill?" she wheezed.

"Dead. I think his neck was broken."

The man on the backboard yelled out, "Fire!"

"What?"

She turned her head to see the first flicker of flame. "We're too late to—"

With a hideous *whump*, a firestorm erupted. *A funeral pyre*, she thought in horror.

Chapter Three

The blast of heat reached them in seconds.

As transfixed as the others, she managed to say, "Back. Let's get farther away."

Kimball reached as if automatically for the backpack.

"Patient first."

He frowned. "I can carry it at the same time."

"It's heavy. Let's move Salazar first. At worst, the bags will be hit by flying…" She petered out. Not coal. Bits of superheated metal? It didn't matter.

Once again, Kimball hoisted one end of the backboard and let her direct where they went. Water shone through the trees. She steered them that way. It seemed…safer, given the inferno behind them. They set down Salazar, and both ran back for the limited stuff she'd been able to pull out.

The uneasiness she'd felt all day made her kneel on the ground with her back to Kimball so she could slide the white hospital bag into her tote. Of course, he wore a weapon in a holster, but she could imagine how he'd react to learn that another gun was just kind of lying around.

In fact, she made sure he didn't see her remove the big black handgun from the bag and push it under the clothes she'd changed out of earlier.

Then she grabbed her two bags and stood. Both hurried back the way they'd come to escape the searing heat. She already felt as if she had a sunburn.

Once they reached the still bound patient, aka captive, Gwen sank to the ground. Kimball set down the pack and knelt beside it, twisted at the waist so he could look back the way they'd come.

"Will the fire spread?" he asked tersely.

Breathless, she said, "I think the couple of trees that are closest will burn. At this altitude, mid-July is more like spring than summer. I hope the vegetation hasn't dried enough to allow the fire to spread. That's…why I wanted to get farther away, though." She could only be grateful that Bill had found a relatively open place to set down.

A pang of grief struck her as she remembered his friendly face.

"You're right. I see a patch of snow," Kimball said in surprise.

"Yes. Um…worse comes to worst, we can immerse ourselves in the lake."

He gave her a sardonic look, for which she didn't blame him. How could they possibly stay under long enough if a full-blown forest fire roared along the shore?

They both watched as fire first crawled then leaped up the tree that had been impaled by the rotor. The crackles and hisses gave her chills. Burning branches plummeted to the ground. Within minutes, however, the flames fell back, having reached barely halfway up the massive trunk.

"Thank God," she murmured.

Kimball let out an audible breath. "Amen."

Seeing the possessive hand he kept on the pack, she nodded at it. "That yours?"

His gaze flicked to her patient, who had probably been watching the fire as well as he could, given his limited range of motion, but who was now watching them. Salazar hadn't said a single word to the DEA agent, she realized, but Kimball hadn't spoken a word to him, either. No matter how adversarial their relationship, that seemed…strange.

In response to her question, Kimball said gruffly, "Yeah. I was planning a short vacation once I delivered Salazar." He actually gave a twisted smile. "Ironically enough, I planned to backpack here in the park. I've never been to the Pacific Northwest before."

What was he going to do, take on the Wonderland Trail? Who knew they'd have an interest in common? She became suddenly and acutely aware of the aches and pains she'd acquired during that rough landing. *Focus*, she told herself.

"Do you have your cell phone? We should both check to see if we have service."

He went very still. "If?"

Had it never occurred to him that they might be entirely isolated in the middle of a wilderness? The pack did look awfully new. Maybe heading into the backcountry was a new hobby for him. Or maybe his hiking had been in regions where tall mountains didn't block phone and even radio service.

Gwen decided to be polite, informing him that cell phones didn't work in much of the park. "I wish I thought Bill had been able to let authorities know we were going down."

"He did." Now he sounded calm, albeit condescending. "Of course he did."

She'd heard chaos, maybe voices, but nothing she could pin down as responding radio traffic.

"Okay," she said slowly, wondering why she

doubted his word. There was surely no question he was the law enforcement agent he'd introduced himself as; Bill and the dispatcher at base would have checked his badge, maybe even made calls to verify his credentials. "Then I guess we just settle in and wait."

She still dug to the bottom of her tote to find her phone. Something flashed in Kimball's eyes at the sight of it. Annoyance that she would still bother checking?

Didn't matter; she had no bars. Maybe a flicker when she turned slightly... No. She'd imagined it.

"This isn't the most comfortable spot," she said. "Let me scout around a little."

Kimball didn't offer to do it for her, but in fairness to him, she hadn't mentioned her suspicion that she had cracked a couple of ribs during the rough fall to earth. Maybe if she had, he'd be more chivalrous. Probably he was afraid Salazar would suddenly throw off the restraints and, despite being recently postsurgery, spring up to take her hostage for his escape.

Right now, her pain felt...distant. Unimportant. She recognized the effect of adrenaline and shock.

Thinking she saw what might be a small open meadow through a nearby cluster of evergreens, she walked toward it. She realized she'd wrapped one arm protectively over her torso, and she was bent forward slightly like an old lady. Rescue couldn't come soon enough for her. She'd just stepped into the trees when she glanced back at the continuing hiss and crackle of the dying fire and heated metal, and instead saw Kimball straddling Rafael Salazar, his hands seemingly around his neck.

She shouted and ran back, her breath wheezing. By the time she reached the two men, Kimball knelt at one side of his prisoner and said, "Thank God! I think he was having a seizure! I was trying to get something in his mouth for him to bite on."

A thick chunk of bark fell from his hand, making his claim credible. But she also saw red prints on both sides of Salazar's neck.

She, too, fell to her knees and laid a hand on her patient's chest. "Mr. Salazar? Are you okay?"

His hands clenched into tight fists at his side. His deep voice had become impossibly gritty. "Now…that you're…here."

Was that a plea she saw in those dark eyes? Did he want her to stay beside him, as if she were his only protection?

"I think we should free him from the backboard," she said. "There's no indication he had a neck or back injury. It would help if he could walk when—"

"No," Kimball said flatly. "I need to keep him under as much restraint as possible." He glanced at the sky streaked with dark smoke. "I expect help will arrive in no time."

His note of smugness disturbed her, contributing to the tingle she recognized as fear. This...wasn't right.

She looked worriedly back at Salazar, seeing his jaw muscles flex. She knew, *knew*, that he wanted to tell her something.

"Well, I for one would like to stretch out on the grass instead of a rocky shore," she said, as lightly as she could manage. "Why don't *you* go check out that meadow beyond the trees? I'm better qualified to be here if Salazar seizes again. It wouldn't take you three minutes."

"Not happening."

Kimball's eyes were brown, too, she realized, but much lighter. Maybe hazel. She couldn't decide.

He knew a lot more about Rafael Salazar than she did—maybe the guy had committed heinous acts as a cartel enforcer, say—but if so, why hadn't he spoken quietly to her so she understood his wariness. As it was, she might not fully understand why she distrusted Agent Kimball, but she did.

It seemed smart not to confront him, so she shrugged. "Oh, fine. If you'll turn your back, I think I'll change clothes."

"Why?" He surveyed her. "What's wrong with that getup?"

"The fabric is designed to protect against fire, not from the cold, and it feels chilly here to me. It'll get colder as the sun lowers." Actually, the sun was high in the sky right now, but it sounded like a good excuse.

"I suppose so." Apparently, Kimball hadn't noticed the bite in the air. She hadn't, either, until she needed to make a production of re-thinking her wardrobe.

She'd apparently been convincing, because he didn't pay any attention while she poked around in her overstuffed tote and dug out a small pile of clothes: a pair of jeans, a T-shirt and the thin fleece jacket she hadn't anticipated needing until they landed in Seattle.

Maybe he really was a gentleman, because he did raise his eyebrow and then ostentatiously turned his back to her. She didn't wait to see if Salazar turned his gaze away, too. Whatever he saw, she felt confident he'd keep to himself.

Still, with two strange men so near, she got dressed in stages as she peeled off the Nomex suit, glad to finally button her jeans and pull on the jacket over the only long-sleeve T-shirt she'd packed. She hoped neither man noticed when she bent over the bag as she laid the now neatly folded flight suit on top of her other possessions in the tote—and eased out the handgun, checked that it was loaded and tucked it into her waistband.

It wasn't comfortable to realize that at this point, she couldn't trust either man. What if no one came for them, and they needed to lean on each other to trek out of what might well be a part of the park lacking roads or trails? She didn't like Kimball, but it was entirely possible that Salazar was playing her with the goal of convincing her to free him.

She had to pretend to explore without taking her eyes off the two of them for more than a minute at a time.

WHEN HE SAW her walking away again, Rafe would have sworn viciously if he didn't have his mouth clamped shut. He'd felt a moment of hope when he saw Gwen handling his gun so competently, then hiding it on her person. Now it appeared that Kimball had convinced her to see him as a threat.

Rafe had no more had a seizure than he had the flu. The fingers wrapped around his throat would have crushed it in short order. The agency rarely had defectors, but Bruce Kimball had to be dirty. And if that was the case, Rafe knew exactly who was paying him.

Out of the corner of his eye, Rafe saw that the woman had disappeared in the trees that weren't more than twenty feet away. The moment she did, Kimball rose abruptly to his feet, looming above him. His teeth showed in a near snarl. "You've been luckier than you deserve so far, but luck always runs out."

"And you're going to see to it." Rafe would have given anything to be able to wrench a single hand free in case Kimball decided to make this up close and personal again.

No such luck. He pulled his gun and aimed it at Rafe's face.

"I'd feel bad if I liked you, but nobody likes glory hogs. Did you really think you were going to bring down the Espinosa family? Sorry, Salazar. They're smarter and more ruthless than you are."

"And you don't feel a single qualm about helping deliver fentanyl to American households in lethal quantities."

A nerve twitched in his cheek. "Maybe I do, but the Espinosas caught me in a bad moment, and now they expect my help when they need it. A man's got to make choices."

Rafe didn't bother asking what Kimball had been doing in that "bad moment." Why bother?

Rafe knew he'd be dead any minute. His almost legendary luck had indeed run out. In one of those strange twists, what bothered him most was the certainty that Kimball intended to kill Gwen Allen, too. What else could he do? Unless he had some slick explanation up his sleeve?

Would she be smart enough to at least pretend to accept that excuse for having to shoot and kill a fully restrained man?

Kimball cast a glance toward the trees. Rafe couldn't even roll into that scumbag's legs in hopes of knocking him off balance thanks to the damn backboard and more secure fastenings than a prison guard could have managed.

"What are you doing?" Gwen called sharply.

Rafe's heart stopped at the same moment Kimball jerked and half turned toward her.

Rafe could barely see her stepping into sight. Chin up, hands at her sides, challenging a federal agent trained to kill under necessity. *Damn it, what was she thinking?*

He yelled, "Run!"

Kimball kicked him and turned his gun toward her.

"You're going to shoot me?" she asked, as if in disbelief.

"Yeah. Too bad." He shrugged. "You weren't supposed to be here, but you had to push."

Kimball was so damn arrogant that his stance

was utterly relaxed. Why not? He expected his audience to be dead in the next minute or two. Rafe had never hated anyone so much before.

Kimball steadied the gun as if he had all the time in the world.

A shot rang out. Rafe waited for death to smash into his head, but instead he heard a second shot, then another, the *crack, crack, crack* obscene in this magnificent country.

Bruce Kimball took a step forward, tripped over Rafe and crashed to the ground as if a logger had felled a magnificent old-growth Douglas fir that made the earth shake when it died.

Stunned, Rafe saw Gwen running forward, a pistol gripped in both hands in firing position.

SHE'D WATCHED ENOUGH cop shows to know it was smart to kick Kimball's weapon a distance away. Then her eyes met Rafe's. "He didn't shoot you?" she asked breathlessly.

"Didn't have a chance."

"Oh, God." Her voice trembled as she looked back at the fallen man. "Do you think…? Is he dead?"

"Yeah," Rafe said hoarsely. "I saw his face when he went down. But…you better check."

Her teeth chattered as she edged closer, leaned over, the gun still in her right hand, and laid two fingers on Kimball's neck.

Then she stumbled back and collapsed onto her butt. "I killed him. I killed a man."

"He didn't give you any choice," Rafe said as gently as he could. "It was you or him."

"You, too," she whispered.

"Definitely me."

Given that she was a person accustomed to making quick decisions in critical situations, she felt weirdly...blank. "What do I do now?"

"Put the gun down," he suggested.

"Oh. Oh, yes." She fumbled to set it on the ground. "Is, um, this yours?"

"I assume so. My boss defied hospital rules and gave it back to me when I was in recovery at the hospital."

She hadn't taken her eyes off the dead man. She was going to see that face, waking and dreaming, for a long time. It wasn't that she hadn't failed to save patients; she'd seen plenty of dead men, women and even children at accident and even disaster sites. But this was different.

I shot and killed a man.

A shudder ran through her.

"Gwen?" Rafe's voice pulled her back to the moment. "We need to move. Can you free me?" he asked.

Still feeling dazed, she looked at him. "I don't understand any of this."

"I...have a good idea. He just filled in a few of the blanks."

"Will you tell me?"

A bald eagle soared far above. With the vast wingspan and bright white head, it was unmistakable. They were common in the Pacific Northwest but always magnificent. She fixated on it, soaring free, because...she didn't want to focus on what had happened.

His voice and words pulled her back. "Yeah," he said. "If it's any consolation, he might have regretted having to kill you."

"Consolation?" she said incredulously. "He didn't sound all that regretful to me. In his worldview, it's my fault that I'm here." She shook her head. "He didn't want me on board. What I don't understand is why Bill—he was the pilot—had apparently agreed to the flight with an injured man and no medical personnel on board. I wanted to think he didn't know what he was doing."

"I'm guessing he didn't, not entirely."

"But...he must have agreed to this...detour." She waved a hand toward the mountain she could no longer see but knew still towered behind rock buttresses and thick evergreen trees.

"Figured pocketing a little money wasn't so bad. Nobody hurt by it."

Her laugh hurt. She curled forward into a tight ball, arms wrapped around her knees.

"He didn't get you, did he?" Rafe sounded alarmed. "I don't see any blood—"

"No. No. I think I suffered some damage during the crash. Like a cracked rib or two."

Which hurt like hell.

She rested her head on her crossed arms and studied him before asking baldly, "Can I trust you?"

Chapter Four

Was she really so naive, she didn't realize how effortlessly he could lie to her? Rafe wondered. It was one of his specialties.

But here and now...he wouldn't. His natural protective side had kicked in anyway, but above and beyond that, this woman had saved his life at least twice already. He owed her. He'd do anything to get her out of this mess alive and well. "You've gotten involved in something worse than you know. Yes, you can trust me. I'm a DEA agent. I don't have my badge or wallet on me—"

"I...think I might have them." She pushed herself to her feet and circled wide around the body to reach that bulging tote bag. After rooting around in it, she produced a white plastic bag with a string closure that he recalled from previous hospitalizations. All that she removed from it was a wallet and a simple billfold. She opened that and had to be looking at his badge.

Finally she lifted her head again. "Now I *really* don't understand."

Even frantic to be released from the re-straints, he understood her doubts. "I've been undercover for the past year. I'd gathered enough information to justify warrants and a cascade of arrests. I was put in a safe house in Yakima to wait for the trial, which could be a year or more away. I expected nothing but ex-cruciating boredom. Somehow, we were be-trayed. One of my guards knew the man he opened the door for. I didn't see him. I'm guess-ing he and the second agent who was there for security are dead. I don't know, except if either had survived, they'd have ID'd the shooter. I crashed out a window, heard sirens as I lost consciousness. The cracked sternum and bro-ken ribs? That's what happens when you're wearing a Kevlar vest and are shot. You sur-vive, but you aren't always happy about it."

"Oh, no," she whispered.

"Next thing I knew, I was in recovery after surgery at the hospital. Like I said, my boss gave me back my gun, badge and wallet, but they must have cut my clothes off. He said some things I didn't comprehend. After that, I was on the helicopter."

"Were you working with Agent Kimball? Or...*was* he an agent?"

"Unfortunately, yes, but based in Chicago. We were in the same office a few years back—

Miami, I think—but I've never worked directly with him. I got a real bad feeling when I heard you say his name."

"You think he's the one your guard recognized."

"Makes sense."

He knew she was having trouble taking all these details in, but he worried about how much time this complicated explanation had eaten up.

"We need to get moving." He had an itch he never ignored, but he hadn't gotten through to her yet. "We're not safe sticking close to the helicopter. I think the pilot was supposed to land somewhere near here, drop Kimball and me off, and fly back. Not sure how he'd have explained that—"

She shook her head. "He was supposed to be flying an empty helicopter to Seattle to be loaned to the base I work out of. We're a lot busier than the team in Yakima, and we have a helicopter that needs serious maintenance. He could have dropped it off as planned, nobody the wiser."

Understanding dawned. "Until you got in the mix."

She explained jumping at the chance for a free ride to Seattle. "Except…there you were."

"I hate to hurry this, but I can't help wondering whether he was expecting a pickup."

"He might have planned to shoot you and then hike out. He did bring the backpack."

"Maybe, but his extracurricular employer might have wanted to see proof that the problem I represented was actually handled."

"We are really exposed." The whites of her eyes showed as her head turned. "We can't be exactly where Bill intended to set down. I mean, this isn't an ideal landing zone, but…"

Rafe followed her gaze to the dark smoke painting an obvious signal in the now mostly blue sky.

He couldn't tell if he'd convinced her at last or if pure instinct had her scooting toward him, her hands reaching for fastenings. Even the anticipation of being freed was almost more than he could stand. This involuntary immobility felt like being buried alive would, or maybe being mummified if you hadn't died yet. Rafe wasn't sure he'd ever be able to lie on his back again, bed covers tucked snugly around him, without feeling the kind of phantom pains amputees did in the missing limb.

Just being able to turn his head was an exquisite relief. To move his shoulders. As she worked her way down, to lift his arms, which promptly cramped.

When he lunged to a sitting position, Gwen fell back, fear on her face.

GWEN SCUTTLED BACK a few feet on the cold ground.

Salazar lifted a hand. "I didn't mean to scare you! I'm sorry. I was just…desperate to move."

She saw only sincerity on his face. The face, she realized even through her fear, that was model handsome, complete with hollows beneath high, sharp cheekbones, a straight, bold nose and a strong jaw darkened by the beginnings of beard growth. It was too bad her willingness to believe and trust was at a low ebb.

Uh-huh, an inner voice commented. *Didn't you already* make *a decision?*

When she turned her head, her gaze fixing unerringly on the man lying face down on the gravelly lakeshore. Dead. Because *she'd* shot and killed him.

Her stomach turned queasily.

What if she'd made a terrible mistake?

He'd admitted he intended to kill her. *You weren't supposed to be here, but you had to push.*

Even so, all she knew was that she'd gotten in the middle of something ugly and maybe convoluted. There might not be a bad guy and a good guy. What if *both* guys were bad?

But Rafael Salazar was still her patient. He'd done or said nothing to rouse her suspicions. She certainly couldn't leave him here to wait for a helicopter sent to pick up Agent Kimball, who had definitely intended to kill him.

She let out a breath and wondered how long she'd been holding it. She felt light-headed. "No, I'm sorry. After everything that's happened, I guess I scare easily."

To her dismay, his smile made him even more handsome. "Understandable. Uh… I think I can get the rest of these straps."

"No, I'll do it." She scooted closer again, then made quick work of freeing him. As he swiveled so that his lower legs lay stretched over the ground, she asked, "How do you feel?"

"Like I've been shot a few times, but I think I can walk."

After what she'd read in his chart, she thought he'd do well to shuffle. Even that would have been impossible if the bullet had struck a little higher and damaged his hip.

Before she could open her mouth, he said, "Except…" He waved at his feet, covered only by hospital socks.

"Oh, no! There weren't any shoes or boots in that bag. At least one of them might have gotten soaked in blood."

He grimaced. "That's…likely. I hate to ask you to rob from the dead, but will you bring me one of Kimball's boots to see if it would fit me?"

Cold—dead?—fingers tripped down her spine, but *practical* probably topped her list of personal qualities. She could do this. She half crawled the short distance, constantly aware of the heat from the helicopter, and studied the boots while trying not to see the rest of the body. No ties, like her hiking boots. These were what were usually called tactical boots. Good sole but flexible, and easy to slide in and out of. She'd seen plenty of cops wearing them. She pulled both off and carried them to Salazar, who said, "These can't be too far off my size."

After shoving his foot into the first, he said, "They're a little too big. If he has extra socks in that pack, the boots should be fine. Some borrowed clothes would be good, too."

Yes, if they had to go on the run in the high mountain wilderness, he'd do better if he wasn't wearing only thin scrubs. She gave thought to whoever had brought his gun and wallet. He couldn't have picked up a change of clothes while he was at it?

She realized she was straining for the distant sound of helicopter rotors. "We should hurry. We can get better organized once we're tucked away."

"You're right." He shoved his other foot in the boot and slowly, torturously got to his feet.

Gwen rose with him and discovered her arms

were out to catch him if he fell. Astonishingly, he didn't, although he swayed initially. She'd guessed he was tall, but at six foot two or three, minimum, he towered over her.

"What do we need to take?" he asked in a rougher voice.

Still half expecting him to go down, she stayed close as she scanned their few possessions.

"Pack, this bag—let me see if I can tie it onto the pack." She suited action to words, securing the trauma bag so she wouldn't have to carry it separately. She looked around. "My tote, your gun—" Which she no longer held, she realized with a tiny burst of panic. No, there it was. She'd set it down after Salazar told her to.

"Kimball's gun, too." He sounded all cop now, no human emotions allowed. "I hope he has clothes in the pack, because I don't think we dare take time to strip him."

"Yes. Okay." Even out of the corner of her eye, she saw that both of Kimball's shirts were bloody. She hurried to pick up both guns, tucking one back in her waistband, putting the other at the top of the tote before she positioned the handles over a shoulder and then hefted the pack onto her back. The weight was reassuring, suggesting that it held both clothes and food.

Unless it was really full of bomb makings or who knew what?

Nice thought.

When Salazar reached out as if he intended to take the tote from her, she stepped away. "Do you go by Rafael?"

"Usually Rafe. I can carry—"

"No, you can't. In fact, you'd better lean on me."

She saw the internal war play out in his dark eyes, but finally he dipped his head.

"I'll keep a hand on your shoulder until I can be sure I'm steady on my feet."

"Good." Gwen didn't even ask which way he thought they ought to go. The sun was too high in the sky to provide any idea of east, west, north or south. A ridge steeper than she thought they could handle rose beyond the lake. Running parallel to it, another ridge, both rocky and treed, put them in…not quite a valley. It wasn't wide enough for that. It was a V. She could see why Bill had seen this as the only option for an LZ.

She wasn't enthusiastic about passing the helicopter because of the heat, and she didn't want to look at the blackened remnants that included a man's body. That left the opposite direction.

She stopped in the act of turning. Even sickened, she had to say this. "What if we put Kimball's body in the helicopter? Or…or right beside it? Would that fool someone into thinking everyone had died in the crash?"

"They probably don't know about you." The man beside her sounded unnervingly thoughtful, but after a moment he shook his head. "I don't think we could pull it off. Not with the gunshot wounds. Anyway, the metal is too hot for us to get near, and even if we were able to put the backboard in, there should be blackened bones. Fire doesn't entirely burn up a body, you know."

She sort of did, since she had a box filled with what was left of her grandmother at home. Even a crematorium, which was *trying* to burn what was left of a human body, couldn't completely succeed.

Grateful that Rafe hadn't jumped on her macabre idea, she felt weak for a minute but hoped he didn't notice.

Still careful not to look at the body sprawled only a few feet away, she led Rafe past it in retracing her earlier path. They needed to find somewhere to hide soon, preferably near enough they could see if a rescue helicopter appeared, and to give Rafe a chance to get into warmer clothes, if there were any, and for her to give him a pain shot.

Once she was back on the job, she was going to have some explaining to do about the quantity of narcotics she'd appropriated without a plan or a coworker to sign off on them. Rules were strict where handling them was concerned.

They were almost to the first line of trees. She looked up to see only grim determination on Rafe's face—and stiff, careful placement of each foot that told her how much pain he had to be suppressing.

Once they reached the trees, Gwen allowed herself a glance over her shoulder. She could no longer see the remains of the helicopter well from here, only the body and the backboard as well as…some litter, she guessed, not sure what it was. She hoped they hadn't left anything important lying around.

If nobody showed up in the next hour or two, she could maybe go back and look more carefully. Also, to strip the man she'd shot of any clothes that didn't have bullet holes in them and weren't stained with blood.

That would be a very last resort, she reassured herself, and felt comforted by the thick cover the copse of feathery evergreen trees provided.

HE'D DO THIS *because he had to*, Rafe thought grimly, but at the moment, he had no idea how. When Gwen had freed him from the restraints, he'd had a burst of euphoria that made him unrealistically optimistic. Now, agony struck with every step, and the pain when he tried to take in a deep breath didn't help. He became aware that he wouldn't have been able to breathe deeply, anyway. His torso was wrapped tightly. Cracked sternum, he reminded himself. Broken ribs. Without the wrap, he'd probably fall to his knees screaming.

He took the next step, only then realizing how tightly he was gripping Gwen's shoulder. As slender as she was, she hadn't so much as flinched, but he was probably bruising her. He loosened his fingers.

"Sorry."

"Hold on as hard as you have to. It'll be worse if you go down."

In so many ways. He squeezed his eyes shut for a minute, picturing what it would feel like to crash to the rocky, uneven ground.

He moved his right leg forward. That was slightly easier, which meant… Left leg. He hoped that was a grunt rather than a groan that came out of his mouth.

"I'm taking us up this side of the ridge, where it isn't too steep," she said, the stress in her voice telling him she knew what he was going through. "I'm hoping it'll seem…unlikely."

This grunt was meant to be agreement. She seemed to take it as such, because the next bit was a struggle. She wedged herself under his good arm, at points getting behind him and pushing.

Rafe's eyes burned from sweat. The too-large boots rubbed and would eventually cause blisters if they kept moving, but he didn't think he'd be able to keep going very long at all.

Yet somehow he did. The strong woman beside him led and supported and sometimes bore almost all his weight, which had to be sixty, eighty pounds more than her finer-boned frame carried. *Conditioning*, he told himself. She must frequently lift one end of a backboard that carried someone a lot larger than him and carry it a distance to the helicopter. He'd be dead if it weren't for her. Again.

Eventually she said, "Let's take a break," and she guided him to a boulder that had a reasonably flat top. Bending to sit was almost worse than walking, but once his butt was supported, he let his head fall forward, closed his eyes and did nothing but breathe through his pain.

She watched him anxiously—he knew she was—but didn't say a word. No perky "You're doing great!" Or "Not that much farther!" which would have been a lie.

What she finally did say was, "I'm going to give you a shot of narcotics."

Real narcotics? Had he misheard?

She went on, "I should have done it sooner, but I have to calculate dose and—"

They hadn't dared sit around.

With a definite groan, he straightened his upper body. "You thought to grab pain meds from a helicopter that was going to blow up any second."

"Last thing I did," she admitted as she rooted in her voluminous tote. "In the helicopter, I intended to ask you about your pain level when I saw the mountain and realized we were so far off course. And… I guess I knew subliminally that we weren't going to be rescued in the next half hour. If you had to move at all, you'd need the good stuff."

He raised his eyebrows.

"Morphine." She asked for his weight and calculated a dose. As he watched, she progressed to drawing a clear liquid from a bottle into a syringe.

Rafe didn't say anything, not wanting to distract her.

"I'm thinking… I won't give you as much as you might get in one dose if you were lounging in a hospital bed. I don't dare take the chance of knocking you out. So you're going to keep hurting." She made a moue of distress.

"But able to stay on my feet. That's a good

decision. Besides—" he eyed the syringe "—I don't want to get addicted."

"No. I have Tylenol in my bag, but that wouldn't help you much for at least a few days."

He only nodded. "Do you want my hip?"

"Well…yes."

He fumbled with the string around the waist, pulled the thin pants down and turned sideways, rolling onto his opposite hip.

The jab came without any warning. The relief that almost immediately rolled through him had him groaning again, his muscles going slack.

"Better?"

"You're an angel of mercy."

She chuckled as she tugged the pants back up but let him tie them at the waist. He felt good enough at this first glorious moment, he wouldn't have minded her fingers playing down there.

Damn. Was he grinning like a fool?

She capped the syringe and replaced it and the bottle in her tote bag. "I think we'd better have a snack. I have some water that's probably warm. We'll undoubtedly come across streams where we can refill the bottle."

What she put in his hand was a Payday candy bar. He ripped it open and took a bite. Salted peanuts and caramel. Did life get any better?

She had chosen an Almond Joy, and both ate

in contented silence, taking sips in turn from her water bottle.

Rafe drew in a deep breath without the hit of pain. The air was so clean; it tasted and smelled of evergreens and something more ephemeral. There were sounds: the rustle of branches high above in a faint breeze, what might be the ripple of water, a birdcall answered by another, but the immensity of the sky and the stunning beauty of the vista around them had the impact of an ancient cathedral.

"I've never been to the Northwest." He grimaced. "Except Yakima, and I barely looked out a window."

"Eastern Washington is spectacular in its own way. The Columbia River Gorge, with crumbling red basalt rim rocks, is magnificent. But the Cascade Range has the most beautiful country in the US, at least."

"I can't argue," he said, taking pleasure in the moment.

Until she stirred. "We haven't come that far. I think we should keep moving, if you're up to it."

What could he say but "Yeah" and let her help him to his feet?

Chapter Five

Before they started out, Gwen did her best to orient herself by pinpointing the base of the column of smoke. It was dismaying to see what a short distance she and Rafe had covered. Not surprising when his every stride had been torturously slow.

Unfortunately, they hadn't crash-landed among old-growth forest, where centuries-old woodland giants would have hidden them well. Plus, that would have given her a better idea of where they were. The trees here were on the small side and seemed to grow in clumps that left quite a bit of open rocky ground and small meadows bright with wildflowers in between. She'd hoped that, in climbing, they'd find something like an overhang that would at least shield them from above.

"How are you?" she asked.

On his feet, Rafe rolled his good shoulder in self-assessment and said, "Better."

Unfortunately, Gwen's rib cage was not feeling better. Maybe she should have given herself some narcotic relief, too, but that would have fuzzed her thinking and would also, as a decision, be hard to defend when she sat down with her supervisor. If worse came to worst—well, she'd think about it then.

Turning her head, she spotted what appeared to be a cliff with tumbled boulders beneath it. That could be a dead end—or give them a place to hide. So she steered Rafe that way.

Apparently, this was her day for denial, because she kept blocking thoughts about everything from her initial decision to get on that cursed helicopter despite her sensible doubts to the crash, the explosion, the—nope. Especially not going there.

Look where you're putting your feet, she instructed herself. *Keep an eye on Rafe's tense face and be aware of his body language. Listen for the distinctive sound of another helicopter. Stay in the moment.*

Everything else could wait for later, including her inconvenient sexual awareness.

Twice she had to detour around crunchy-topped, gleaming white snow fields to be sure they didn't have a clear line of footprints. If he noticed the long ways around, it wasn't apparent.

He was able to reach with one hand for branches

to pull himself up a few feet, taking some of his weight off her shoulders. That was an improvement. Still, she had a feeling his thoughts weren't trying to scatter like a covey of quails the way hers were, but rather were grimly focused on the next moment. Maybe on-the-job experience had taught him an intense focus. Either way, she'd bet he was thinking about nothing but the next step.

Except then he spoke up in a gritty voice, surprising her.

"Do you know where we are in the park? I assume we *are* in the national park?"

"I think we're still in the park. We were awfully close to the mountain not that long before things went wrong. As for where…only sort of. I mean, the glimpse I had was out the left window, which would put us on the east side, except we could have been curving around the north side, depending on where Bill and Kimball had agreed to set down. Also, I have no idea how much time passed or how far we traveled after Bill claimed the alarm had gone off. And, well, the sun isn't any help yet."

"Hard to set a route, then."

Matter-of-fact, but with a growly undertone that spoke of pain.

"Unfortunately, yes. Depending on where we came down, we could be near a heavily used trail or even an entrance to the park." She hated to say this. "We could also be miles from help."

"Kimball wouldn't have wanted anyone to see the helicopter set down."

Yes, he was right. Had he and Bill plotted an especially remote part of the park?

Except…logic said if Kimball had intended to walk away with that pack on his back, he'd have planned for the original LZ to be within a reasonable distance of a trail. She didn't point that out. Speculation wouldn't get them very far.

Rafe didn't say any more for a long time. She didn't blame him, given that they were scrambling more than walking at the moment.

During a brief break to catch their breath, she decided a little optimism might help. "Once we look through the pack and see what resources we have, we might be better able to make an educated choice for our next move."

Surely this grunt wasn't meant to dismiss her near perkiness but was just the best he could do at the moment.

It felt as if they'd been on their way for an hour or more, but she suspected the time was a lot shorter than that. She saw what she'd been looking for, though—a boulder leaning against another that created something close to a shallow cave beneath. Soil and small pebbles made a nearly flat spot.

"This way," she said.

She nudged. He changed his path. When they arrived and she stopped him with a hand on his arm, he stared straight ahead like a robot that had been shut down.

Gwen dropped the tote and lowered the backpack to the ground, wishing it wasn't bright red, then touched Rafe's arm. "Let's sit down."

She could tell what an effort it took him to turn his head and assess their surroundings, but he nodded finally and said, "Good."

He didn't argue when she knelt, put his hand on her shoulder and said, "Slow and easy."

The last part of his descent was more of a fall, but he landed safely on his butt, leaned his head against the gritty rock to one side and exhaled a breath slowly.

Studying him worriedly, she touched his forehead. Was it too warm, or was her hand cold? She pressed it to her own cheek and couldn't tell. Knowing wouldn't help since the best she could do if he had a fever was Tylenol.

Well, she could look under his dressings for signs of infection, but she had no antibiotics to give him and, at the moment, didn't even have any more water for him to swallow a pill.

"Still no helicopter," he said hoarsely. "Maybe you were right."

"About the hiking-out thing?"

"Yeah."

Gwen told him her earlier thoughts.

"Too close to a trail, he'd have risked witnesses," he commented.

She nodded. "No matter what, I may have chosen the wrong direction."

"No." His big hand caught hers. "Smart."

"Okay." She closed her eyes and tipped her head sideways to rest on his shoulder. Her body felt compressed, even her bones scrunched. She'd carried too much weight, but now they could rest. There was no reason they couldn't stay here for a while. Maybe even overnight. They both might feel better tomorrow.

She gave herself what had to be five minutes before she straightened.

"Cross your fingers. Let's find you something better to wear."

He did cross his fingers, and she pulled a laugh out of somewhere.

She unfastened Velcro and explored. Rafe was bent over the pack as eagerly as she was.

RAFE WAS INCREDIBLY grateful when they found a couple changes of clothes in the pack, as well as three pairs of socks. He removed the boots and showed Gwen the red places on his feet close to forming blisters.

"Try two pairs of socks when we move on," she decided. "I wish we had some moleskin, but if you're still uncomfortable, I can figure out something else to cut up to protect those places."

Even one pair of socks warmed his feet. The fact that she knelt in front of him to put them on felt…good.

Apparently, Kimball really had intended to backpack, whether here at Rainier or elsewhere, because the pack disgorged a small stove with an extra fuel canister, a number of freeze-dried meals, purifying tablets for water, bags of dried fruit and nuts, and energy bars.

"This will keep us for a while," Gwen said with satisfaction. "I have some energy bars in my bag—I never go anywhere without any— and more candy bars."

"Sweet tooth?"

Her smile lit her face. "I'm not shy about admitting it. You?"

"I'd say no, except that Payday really hit the spot."

She chuckled, dug some more and laid out a miscellany of things: a lighter and matches, a folding knife with additional tools, a tarp and cord that could be used to rig a cover in case of rain, a compact pair of binoculars and a couple of magazines for Kimball's handgun.

"Did he know guns are banned in the park?"

Rafe raised an eyebrow at her, and she blanched. Frowning, he laid his hand on her arm. "I didn't mean it like that."

Suddenly, she started to shake. "I never thought I'd kill anybody."

She'd been so tough, he'd forgotten how disturbing today's events must have been for her. "You shot him in self-defense." He hoped his voice conveyed comfort. "Do you regret that choice?"

"No. No. It's just—" face pinched, Gwen hugged herself "—I couldn't let him kill us, but... I chose my profession to save lives," she said finally.

"I can see that." Damn. He wanted to put his arm around her but wasn't sure how she'd take that. "Gwen, look at me."

She did. In fact, she searched his eyes in a way that shook him, as if she saw deep into his darkest memories, the ones that turned up in an occasional nightmare.

"You did save my life," he reminded her. "Remember that. Isn't that your job?"

Her forehead creased as she visibly tried to reconcile the two concepts. "I just...never thought..."

"Why did you become a paramedic?"

"I became a nurse and then wanted to do more. I've always... I guess you could say I enjoy adrenaline. I mean, I don't do extreme sports or anything like that—"

"I'm relieved to hear it," he said dryly.

"But my rotation in the ER made other kinds of nursing seem dull. I got certified as an EMT and worked on an ambulance for a while, went back to the ER, then studied to become a paramedic."

"You still haven't said why. Were either of your parents in the medical field?"

She went so still that he suspected she'd quit breathing. He'd unwittingly touched on a sore place. Was this something she didn't talk about?

"Rafe," she said suddenly, her hand shooting out to grip his forearm hard. "Do you hear that?"

He did. Only his attention on her had kept him from noticing the distant sound of a plane flying low or a helicopter.

They both knew which it would be.

"Gun," he said, and she dug quickly in her tote and produced Kimball's Glock, the same model as his. Not surprising, since agents were encouraged to carry one of a couple of Glocks. Even with the pain in his shoulder, Rafe did a quick check to be sure it was ready to fire.

She produced the binoculars, too. Smart thinking. "Maybe…maybe somebody spotted the smoke, and it'll be a rescue helicopter."

She was whispering for no logical reason, but he understood why.

He took the binoculars, lifting them to his eyes and adjusting them until the vicinity of the crash, visible from here only by the smoke, snapped into sharp focus.

"There," Gwen said.

He saw it, too.

What emergency flight helicopters he'd seen were clearly marked. Big numbers on the tail, logo of the organization operating it on the side, paint job white or a bright color. The goal was to be visible. This one was black with a white stripe. Law enforcement? But even when it got close enough and he could examine it carefully, he saw no logo, and the FAA required numbers on the tail were present but small enough he couldn't quite make them out.

He handed the binoculars to Gwen and let her study it. She worked in the area and must see helicopters belonging to any number of emergency responders, sightseers, and search and rescue groups.

She shook her head. "It has to be private."

They watched it drop low and circle the crash site. Even from this distance, the noise was near deafening. It appeared to settle on the ground for what had to be five minutes. Undoubtedly, someone had gotten out to identify the dead man and try to figure out what had happened. Then it rose again, tipping to one side to curve into the beginning of a circle as if it were turning back the way it had come. Except it flew in a complete circle, then another, each enlarged.

"Search grid," he murmured. "They know at least one person is missing."

Her fingers bit into his arm.

"Let's pull back under cover as much as we can manage," he added, grateful when she didn't argue. In fact, she used her head and pushed the too-bright red pack to the very back of their V-shaped hideout, poking her flower-print tote bag after it. Finally, he and she shuffled backward until they were crouched, Rafe holding the gun in his right hand but propping that arm up with his stronger left hand.

The helicopter got louder. It passed frighteningly close to them. Rafe didn't try to use the binoculars, afraid a flash of light off a lens would give away their location. It didn't slow, though, only continued in another wide circle, this time passing above and behind them.

Finally, they could no longer see it or, after a few more minutes, hear it.

Gwen whimpered. "That was—"

"Scary as hell," he agreed.

She'd been the one shaking earlier, but he felt a tremor in his own hands now. In one way, he'd expected this. In another, he hadn't understood how difficult escape would be with him in such bad shape and with them having absolutely no idea which direction to go to find even an occasionally traveled trail. And there had to be *some* roads in the park, too, didn't there?

"Do you…think it'll come back?"

Rafe mulled over how to answer. Clearly, the enforcement arm of the traffickers had landed, seen the dead DEA agent they'd suborned and been forced to assume that Rafe had overpowered Kimball, shot him and gone on the run. They had no way to know he had help. They might wonder if he'd been injured as badly in the first place as they had been led to believe.

Problem with that was, they'd set up a pretty elaborate operation with only one goal: killing Rafe, the federal agent who'd fooled them well enough to gather information on their operations to bring down significant parts of their organization. Their goal was to keep him from ever testifying. A judge and jury needed him there in front of them to verify and elaborate on the evidence he'd collected. What the men who'd been given the job of getting rid of him had found was the body of their dirty agent.

The scene suggested Rafe was still alive and therefore a threat to some higher-ups in the cartel.

How could they go back to the bosses and admit he'd gotten away? That kind of major screwup wouldn't be accepted with any understanding.

"I wish you'd never gotten involved in this," Rafe told Gwen honestly, "but I wouldn't have a chance without you."

"So, that's a yes," she said slowly.

He had to think back to her original question and nodded. "My best guess is that they hadn't come prepared to drop any men to hunt for me. I think the pilot has gone back to pick up some armed trackers."

"I thought we could spend the night here." She sounded sad.

Seeing her exhaustion and stress and shock, Rafe wished he could spare her. "We're too near the crash site," he said bluntly. "We need to get as far away as we can before they come back."

She wrinkled her nose at him, straightened her shoulders and said with determination, "Then let's not waste any time."

He couldn't possibly have gotten any luckier in a partner, Rafe thought again, then hoped she didn't see his wince.

Rafe wasn't much for introspection. He

planned, he stayed fit in preparation for whatever would be thrown at him, he relied on his lightning-fast reaction time and, yeah, he knew one of his strengths was the subconscious calculations that he called gut feelings.

He compartmentalized, too, as most people in his line of work probably did. Had to shut bad experiences, tragedy, ugly scenes away. For the first time, it struck him that the consequence might be self-centeredness. He thought of himself as a compassionate man; he'd give his life for that of an innocent, no hesitation. But day to day…he calculated in terms of how events and people would help or hinder *him* on the job.

That's what he'd just done. Gwen Allen was a gutsy woman who improved his chances of escaping this disaster and making it to court to bring down a lot of bad guys.

But what would the fallout be for *her*—assuming both of them in fact survived? Keeping her alive had been a high priority for him, but was that enough?

Chapter Six

Gwen had set aside a map of Mount Rainier National Park found among Kimball's belongings. After laying out a change of clothes for Rafe, she said, "Let me know if you need me," and then turned her back to give him privacy to strip and get dressed. Over her shoulder, she added, "Oh! Or if you see any blood on your dressings."

While he was changing only a few feet away, she completely unfolded the map to scrutinize it. No, she wasn't delusional enough to think Kimball would have marked a big red X at the rendezvous point, although people did do things like that, didn't they? After all, he had no reason to believe anyone but him would get their hands on the map.

It wasn't completely pristine; there was enough wear and tear that she could tell the map had been opened a few times, and whoever had done it—Kimball—had struggled to refold it correctly so that it didn't tear or end up a wadded mess.

Rustles and scrapes came from behind her. Rafe's arm brushed against her. Gwen winced at some pained sounds, even as she pictured his powerful body unclothed. She'd seen enough of his muscles to know there had to be a lot more of them. She wanted to slap herself for even thinking like that. He was still her patient! She'd taken care of well-built guys before and not felt even an instant of attraction.

She let out a breath. Surely he'd let her help pull the shirt over his injured arm and shoulder.

Quit thinking about him seminaked, she ordered herself, bending to search the map.

Unfortunately, there were no helpful ink or pencil circles, Xs or margin notes to grab her attention. What was spread in front of her was just a topographical map published by National Geographic identical to one she owned, beautifully detailed, but not giving her a clue where their helicopter had come down. If only she had caught a better glimpse of the mountain before the clouds closed in!

She frowned. Since they'd gone on the run, she should have paid more attention to the foliage, the trees in particular. Pines were more common on the dryer east side, for example. Thinking about it now, she didn't remember noticing one, although her attention had been split too many ways.

She could identify different elevation zones because some species or types of trees lived only at lower elevations while others only appeared higher up. At the moment, she didn't believe they were at the subalpine elevation of 4,500 feet above sea level or higher, but they might not be much below that. In fact...

"Where are you from?" she asked Rafe.

There was a startled silence behind her. "We're going to exchange background info right now?"

She rolled her eyes. "No, I'm thinking about elevation. I've been puffing and panting more than usual, thinking my exercise regime doesn't cut it, but it's occurred to me that we might be at a high enough elevation that it would be normal for us to find it harder to breathe. Unless you're from somewhere like Denver..."

"No. I grew up in Southern California, and with the DEA, I've been transferred several times, but Miami, Houston and San Diego are essentially at sea level. Probably Chicago, too. Damn. This means there's another reason we're moving so damned slow."

"Afraid so."

Too bad their current elevation didn't help in identifying their location.

She leaned over the map again. The distinctively parallel ridges rising to each side of that narrow valley had worried her. She shouldn't generalize from them—her view had been pretty limited—but there were a number of places in the park where the land folded that way. A lot of those areas tended to be devoid of roads or trails because the terrain was so difficult.

Rafe said grittily, "I could use a hand."

He'd managed to pull on the heavy-duty cargo pants but had gotten stuck halfway taking off the surgical scrub top.

"Oh, no!"

He was so tangled that she grabbed the pocket knife and cut it off him. It wasn't anything he'd want to wear again, anyway. Of course a wide, white wrap supported his ribs. Somehow, she hadn't been picturing it. Rafe had a beautifully muscular chest with warm copper-brown skin and a dark dusting of hair, and powerful arms and broad shoulders. It was even better than she'd imagined. She wanted to touch him, but the lack of fresh blood on the dressing around his upper arm and over his shoulder meant she didn't have an excuse.

Considering they were on the run for their lives and he was seriously injured, what was she *thinking*?

"Um, let's see." She picked up the T-shirt like she'd never seen one before, finally deciding to slip it over the arm on his bad side, then maneuver to get his head and other arm in it.

She gently pulled it down, reluctant to hide that lovely male body, but reached for the Polartec fleece quarter-zip.

Only when he was fully dressed did she let herself meet his eyes. If there was a knowing glint in them, she wasn't acknowledging it.

"Boots," she declared, and helped him put them on.

He stamped each foot, then sighed. "Anything on the map?"

"Sad to say, no X marks the spot."

He leaned closer, and she pointed out some remote areas with the kind of ridges—or were they really mountains?—that might fit. There was a large area west of the Chinook Scenic Byway, for example, in which no roads or trails were displayed. From there, it wouldn't be that many miles to the highway—if they could get there at all. And they'd have to head east instead of the generally westward route she'd chosen. Those folds were more than ridges, she saw; they were definitely mountains over six thousand feet in elevation, many named.

The Chenius Mountain area, too, was devoid of trails. But really, by its very nature, the land surrounding a volcano this size consisted of pleats of land formed in some cases by glaciers, or at least the runoff of melting ice and snow. In other words, she had no more idea where they were than she'd had before she opened the map.

Rafe's dark gaze rested on her as she folded the map and put it away. She wasn't sure she wanted to know what he was thinking. Surely they'd eventually come upon a view of the mountain that would offer her guidance, but that was no help right now.

Look for the fastest path, she told herself, the one that would let them open up some distance, but still have thick groves of trees or rocky ground that might offer an overhang or the like to hide them. They'd have to avoid being in the open as much as they could, she realized; flower-strewn meadows made for more pleasant walking but were dangerous for them. Searchers might be on foot, but when the helicopter reappeared, it could hunt them from the air again, too.

"I guess right now, we just need to cover as much ground as we can while never being far from someplace we can duck to get out of sight."

"I agree," he said. "Except it would be ideal if we had a sight line when that helicopter comes back."

More reason to go up rather than scrambling along the side of the ridge. She could only hope it didn't get too steep.

Somehow he shoved himself to his feet, his good shoulder braced against the side of a boulder to give him support.

Relieved he hadn't asked for another shot of morphine, Gwen loaded herself down again even as she realized she had no idea how to determine intervals between shots. She didn't wear a watch, although she might rethink that after this adventure.

One more thing she'd have to guess at.

Those dark eyes raked her. "Do you have any idea how much I hate seeing you loaded down like a pack animal while I'm strolling along empty-handed?"

"*I* don't have two gunshot wounds," she pointed out tartly. "I carry this much weight when I'm backpacking, which I do for *fun*, and regularly for short periods on the job."

He grunted, his favorite sound.

She laughed at him and saw the beginnings of a reluctant, sexy grin.

"I think…this way." She pointed.

MAYBE HALF AN hour along, Rafe's feet balked. Since the rest of him was in agreement, he managed to grind out, "Break."

"What?" Gwen turned, saw the expression on his face and looked around. "If it's not too rotten, we can sit on that fallen tree."

He plodded that far, sinking down with enormous relief. She followed suit and moaned.

After a minute, he became aware she was watching him sidelong.

"Something on your mind?" he asked.

"I keep remembering. You know?"

He did, but that was part of the difference between them. He sought answers that might be of use; she might be stuck on the two deaths they'd walked away from. He had no idea whether he should discourage that or encourage her to talk it out.

He settled for making an inquiring sound.

"Back in the helicopter," she said in a rush, "I heard something strange just before it started spinning. What if we crashed because Kimball knocked Bill unconscious or even killed him *before* we landed?"

Although Rafe hadn't thought about it, that seemed entirely possible to him. At some point Kimball would have realized that Gwen's inclusion meant Bill couldn't live, either.

"What would make him think *he* could land a helicopter?" she begged.

He hated seeing the turmoil in those beautiful eyes. "DEA agents aren't like Navy SEALs," he explained, "who claim to be able to operate anything from a submarine to a NASA rocket." The couple of SEALs he'd met had been full of themselves. "But depending on what kind of investigations we've been involved in, we develop skills. I'm good with boats." He'd even piloted an illegal submersible. "We do have helicopter pilots. Kimball might have been one."

"If so, he chose a terrible time to take over."

"He was plenty arrogant. That isn't necessarily what happened, though."

After an interval, she said quietly, "Poor Bill."

"He chose a slippery slope."

Gwen didn't say anything. A minute later, without another word, they rose and set out again.

As they walked, he heard birdcalls and an odd shrill whistle he couldn't identify but felt sure wasn't human, saw the flick of a squirrel tail. Even he recognized the *rat-a-tat-tat* as a woodpecker.

Their next stop was made when crossing a small creek carrying snowmelt down to the lakes and rivers at a lower elevation. Just above them, a small waterfall dropped no more than five feet. The water sparkled as it danced and tumbled over moss-covered rocks, ferns clustered to each side. Thirsty as they were, Gwen recommended against drinking it without treatment. They filled her bottle and the empty one from the pack and dropped in the purifier tablets Kimball had thoughtfully provided for safe drinking. According to her, there were several nasty pathogens in what appeared to be pristine high mountain water.

Rafe slipped when stepping over the rock-strewn stream, twisted his ankle but found that Kimball's boots were more or less waterproof. Good thing, because he'd have hated to squelch as well as struggle for his footing over a rough side slope. He took a few cautious steps before deciding he hadn't done any significant damage.

He'd about hit his limit again, but he kept his jaws clamped together so he couldn't admit it when he heard something that made the hair on the back of his neck rise.

"Oh, no," Gwen breathed.

Good thing helicopters were such noisy machines. He and Gwen had enough advance warning to plunge into a stretch of woodland that wasn't as thick as he'd have liked but should serve to hide them.

Once he'd knelt and she crouched amidst some rare understory vegetation with purple berries, further shielded by low, almost feathery branches of an evergreen, he calculated it might have been an hour and a half to two hours since the helicopter left.

Sure enough, the damn thing started by flying over the same territory it had earlier and then expanding what wasn't quite a systematic grid but was close. On its last pass, it nearly went right overhead again.

But finally, it turned back and presumably set down, although Rafe could no longer see the thing.

Damn it, he *needed* to see what he and Gwen were up against, so instead of staying put, he pushed to his feet again. "I'm going to try to find a viewpoint."

"Wait! I'll come, too."

He wanted to say no, but right now, she was stronger than he was, so he waited until she'd shrugged off the pack. They were too far away to worry about being heard but had to be careful not to pop out too precipitously into the open.

All he could tell for the next few minutes was that the helicopter was still there, although the pilot never shut down the engines. Rafe must have subconsciously kept in mind where the crash site was, because this time, he led the way until he saw a rock promontory ahead. It took some effort to lower himself to his belly and crawl forward. Gwen stayed behind him.

He'd put the binoculars around his neck earlier. If too many tall trees blocked their view, they were screwed, but Gwen's strategy of gaining elevation was the best they could have done.

He reached the edge of the rocky outcrop, braced himself with the elbow on his good side and raised the binoculars. There was the smoke, a dark trail diminished now but still obvious. Maybe no longer visible from any great distance. Yeah, he could see the whirling blades on the helicopter…and movement beside it. Two men— no, there was another pair. All wearing green camouflage and equipped with hefty packs.

No rifles to be seen, but he supposed they wanted to look like your average backpackers if they happened upon any climbers or hikers.

Even so, he hoped no park ranger met up with them and asked too many questions. He doubted they'd bothered with backcountry permits.

One man lifted a hand, and the helicopter rose again, banked and returned the direction it had come.

Rafe wondered if Bruce Kimball's body was now in the belly of the helicopter. Had to be. If legitimate search and rescue should find the crash site, questions about a dead man with bullet wounds could prove awkward.

Rafe watched the foursome until his eyes burned, then squirmed backward. He looked at Gwen.

"Four men," he said, "wearing camouflage and carrying dark green packs. They're being discreet but no doubt have some firepower tucked away."

Her eyes closed for a moment, and then she retreated all the way to where she'd left their pack. He followed, rising to his feet at the end.

The only positive he could think of was that the two of them were also armed, and she'd taken out Bruce Kimball with a deadly accurate shot. Later, he'd have to ask Gwen how and why she'd learned to shoot like that, especially given her dedication to saving lives rather than taking them.

On the negative side, the two of them currently moved at the speed of a banana slug. They also weren't dressed to blend. He doubted either of them had paid attention to whether they were trampling vegetation when they set out. For all he knew, they'd all but laid down an airport runway.

"Let's move while we can," he suggested.

Once she'd hefted the damn pack on her back, Rafe bit off another groan as he pushed himself to his feet again. His body instantly revolted, muscles cramping into white-hot knots of agony. For a minute, he had to bend over at the hips, hands braced on his thighs, and do nothing but wait and try to breathe. Gwen hovered beside him, anxious. She reached for him, hesitated then took her hand back, obviously knowing there was nothing she could do.

Except give him more morphine, but he refused to ask for it. He had to push those intervals out as long as he could. For starters, he didn't know how much of the stuff she had. He didn't want to become too dependent, either, and he especially didn't want a drug scrambling his brain. Things were likely to get worse before they got better.

"I'm okay," he said roughly, straightening.

With an uneasy glimpse back the way they'd come, she started out again, bowed beneath the weight of the big pack. He shuffled after her.

THE PRIMAL INSTINCT that had steered Gwen toward higher ground despite the harder going kept flaring. She wanted to *see* behind and below them. They might initially have laid a trail a Scout could follow, which meant now sticking to rocky ground as much as possible would be smart.

Divorcing herself from her aching body, she brooded. This whole thing kept escalating. Four men were prepared to spend however much time was necessary to hunt down her and Rafe.

She'd thought that the moment when she realized Kimball was trying to strangle Rafe was the worst—until he'd turned his gun on her and she'd had to make such a horrible choice. Now she understood this might never end.

The whole elaborate scheme had been meant to make Rafe vanish from the face of the earth. That wouldn't have been hard to do in a wilderness where a tossed body would have been down to bones in no time, and those probably dragged off by animal activity.

She was the one who'd been the monkey wrench in the works. Next time...

Rafe would be dead if it weren't for me, she thought. *Although Bill would be alive.*

Only she no longer believed that. Could Kimball really have let Bill fly on to Seattle as planned and trusted he'd stay mum about his part in all this?

Gwen had to wonder what Rafe's boss at the DEA was doing right now, too. Even if he'd flown back to the office, wherever that was, he'd have learned at some point that Rafe was no longer convalescing in the hospital, that in fact he was missing.

Figuring out where he'd gone initially should, on the face of it, be a no-brainer. The hospital wouldn't have handed over a patient to just anybody. Kimball must have flashed credentials at the hospital as well as at the air rescue base. An ambulance crew had transported Rafe to the airfield and loaded him into the helicopter. Plenty of people knew what had happened to Rafe, up to the point when the helicopter took off.

Except, Kimball almost had to have used a badge with a fake name. He sure wouldn't have wanted to be on record. If that was so, why did Bill have his real name? She puzzled over that one, until she thought, *What if Bill recognized him?* Military helicopter pilot, DEA agent— they might have encountered each other at some time in the past.

If that was the case, Bill wouldn't have survived to fly the helicopter to Seattle no matter what.

Well, the helicopter never did arrive in Seattle. A search should have been instigated on both ends. Unfortunately, the initial focus would have been the expected route, not the scenic detour Bill had been paid off to take.

Whatever the scenario, she saw an inevitable outcome.

If Kimball had used a false name earlier, as that seemed logical—could he have stolen some other agent's badge?—that would confuse any attempt to find out who was involved in kidnapping Rafe.

"Let's take another break," she said.

His expression didn't change, but he nodded. Once they were seated, she handed him the water bottle and then dug in her tote for the bottle of Tylenol. When she gave him several pills, he swallowed them without question—for what good they'd do.

When her turn came to drink, she took some Tylenol, too.

"Do you think they'll split up?" she asked after a minute.

"Makes sense." He paused. "Maybe search in pairs."

What if they were able to stay in touch with SATCOM radios, too?

"You said you saw your boss at the hospital," she said abruptly.

He gave her a surprisingly sharp look from those brown eyes, given his exhaustion and pain. "Yes."

"Well, do you trust him?"

His silence lasted long enough to make her uneasy.

"Yeah. He's never given me reason not to." The slowness of his response told her this wasn't the first time he'd wondered. "He did give me back my weapon."

"In recovery at the hospital. That's…surely not usual."

"No. I was too out of it to think it through, but now I wonder…"

She wondered, too. About a lot. "If we had

internet access we might be able to find out whether your bodyguards died."

"Unless the whole incident was buried."

"Why would authorities—" *Oh, heck*, she could think of reasons. The city of Yakima may never have known that a federal law enforcement agency had set up a safe house there. They wouldn't have appreciated not being informed, especially after a gun battle erupted in a peaceful neighborhood. Or… "If one of the other men is alive…"

"I think that's unlikely, but I can hope."

She watched as a bird—a bright blue Steller's jay—sidled along a branch, head tilting one way and then the other as *he* watched her. After a moment, she said wryly, "I can't decide if I wish I'd bought a ticket on that Greyhound bus or am glad I didn't."

Rafe's hand caught hers. "You know my vote."

The warmth and strength of his grip was more comforting than it ought to be. She clasped his hand in return, and neither moved for a long time.

Chapter Seven

"Can you go on?" Gwen asked.

A flash of anger showed in Rafe's eyes. "I should be asking you that. You're having to do all the work."

Feeling a little grumpy herself, she retorted, "Here we go again. Is this because I'm a woman?"

"No!" He glared at her. "It's because you're half my weight."

"That's an exaggeration."

"And you're injured, too."

She sighed. "I don't think my ribs are broken, or they'd hurt more than they do." Which was bad enough, but she wasn't telling him that. "They're maybe cracked or just bruised. Later, I'll have you help me wrap them."

His jaw tightened still more.

"Have you forgotten that you were *shot* multiple times last night? That you had surgery *early this morning*? Were still woozy enough not to know what was happening to you when you got tied hand, foot and the rest of your body and then were kidnapped from the hospital? And, hey, a few hours later, *we fell out of the sky?*" She was practically shouting.

He stared for a minute longer, then let his head sink forward.

Gwen took a chance and patted his broad back. "I understand."

Lifting his head, he growled, "You had to do that?"

"Express sympathy?"

"You should have just slapped me and marched away. Let me catch up if I could."

She studied him. "Is it really so bad to lean on someone else a little?"

"Sometimes I work with partners. Needing to trust someone else isn't the same as feeling useless. Useless gets you killed in my profession."

Uneasiness had begun creeping over her. "Can we walk and argue at the same time?"

"Did you hear something?"

"No. Just…"

"Yeah." He pushed himself up. "Put the damn tote bag over my good shoulder." His eyes narrowed to slits when she hesitated.

As exhausted as she was, not carrying the surprisingly heavy and awkward bag would be an enormous relief. Once they stopped for the night, she should go through it. There might be things she could ditch. She did as he asked, then shrugged into the pack and forced herself to straighten.

"We don't have to argue," he said, as this time they fell into step together.

"No. Just..." He'd hate this, but she wanted to say it, anyway. If only once. "What you've succeeded in doing, essentially rising from a hospital bed postsurgery, is next to miraculous. You know that, don't you? And...if I were out here alone, I'd be a lot more scared than I am."

No, she'd probably still be sitting shell-shocked and sniveling beside the body of the man she shot and killed. Because of Rafe, she'd had to pull herself together and remember who she was: a strong, capable woman who wasn't going to let some drug-trafficking scum kill her *or* her patient.

HE'D APOLOGIZED FOR his momentary breakdown and then spent what was probably the next half hour trying to figure out what had triggered it.

It was true he hated being helpless. Most people probably did, and anyone who served in the military or law enforcement more than most. Not being at the top of your game equated to vulnerability. And, yes, that was certainly true right now. If he hadn't been so seriously wounded, *he'd* be carrying the pack, and he and

Gwen would be moving a lot faster. That she had to travel at the speed of a patient shuffling up and down the hospital corridor gripping an IV pole was his fault.

Hell, it was his fault she'd gotten mixed up in this in the first place.

Except that wasn't so. It was Bruce Kimball's. If he hadn't sold his soul to the devil, there never would have been an attack on the safe house. Rafe would still be resigned to the months of tedium to come. Gwen would have made her way to Seattle, and Rafe would never have met her. Bill the pilot wouldn't have been tempted, and he'd be alive.

And above and beyond all that, if an organization of morally bankrupt human beings weren't determined to profit by providing an incredibly dangerous substance to relative innocents, none of this would have happened.

A powerful, intensely addictive opioid, fentanyl could be produced cheaply and mixed into recreational drugs, in some cases increasing the high but too often killing the user, who wasn't even aware that an unknown, deadly substance was in their favorite products from the local dealer, or the pills labeled as painkillers or antianxiety meds or even muscle relaxants bought off the internet. If the quantity of fentanyl was too high, people died quickly. It was as simple as that. Fentanyl was currently considered to be the leading cause of death for Americans aged eighteen to forty-nine. It had zoomed to the top of the Drug Enforcement Administration's priorities.

The cartel Rafe had inserted himself into was based in Mexico, but the organization had tentacles spread throughout their chief market, the US.

Rafe had never hated the people he was investigating as much as he had the Espinosa family and their underlings. People smuggling cocaine knew it was illegal, that it was addictive, but it didn't have as much possibility of killing someone when they took their first snort. Every single person involved in manufacturing and trafficking fentanyl knew the risks that even one hit could kill. They didn't care.

By the end, Rafe had been desperate to answer every question he could, collect proof that would send the maximum number of these creeps to prison for long periods. He wanted to be done, to breathe clean air again, to allow himself to sleep deeply without a knife and gun under his pillow.

The idea of a year of stultifying boredom hadn't excited him, but that was the price he'd known he would have to pay. Settled into the safe house, at least initially, he'd been glad for some downtime.

Who knew this was the closest he'd get to a vacation? Struck by the irony, he lifted his gaze from his feet to take in the grandeur surrounding him, puffs of cloud crossing the brilliantly blue sky and the small yellow flowers growing from gritty soil between rocks. Then he absorbed the sight of the woman in front of him, her fat caramel-colored braid swaying over her slim back and her endless legs and a perfectly shaped rear that made his fingers twitch.

I'm damn lucky, he realized—which didn't shut down his fear that this gutsy woman might end up dying beside him.

He almost walked into her. Had she seen or heard something?

"The sun is dropping," she said. "At least the sun confirms we're northeast of Rainier. Probably in the park, but I can't be positive. There's a protected wilderness outside the park boundary. Anyway, we should look for someplace to stop for the night."

He tipped his head again. Yes, the sun was lower than it had been, but the sky was bright. This didn't look like sunset to him.

"If we can keep going even for another hour..."

She shook her head. "Night falls fast in the

mountains. Then the temperature plummets just as fast, even at this time of year. Besides, we both need a serious rest. I keep stumbling and my knees want to crumple and—"

He squeezed her upper arm. "You're right. I've gotten so all I do is stare at my feet to be sure I don't misstep. A grizzly could come roaring at us, and I wouldn't notice."

Her smile brought life back to her face. "No grizzlies in this part of the state."

He grimaced in return. "One small blessing."

Transfixed by her laugh—by her *ability* to laugh—he had to be staring. Her eyes widened, and she backed up a step or two.

"Well, let's, um, check out those trees over there."

"Good idea," he managed to say, and tore his gaze from her.

As EXHAUSTED AS she was, the sound of falling water wove into her consciousness like orchestra music appropriate to the beauty around them. Gwen clambered above a small patch of snow, Rafe right behind her, the noise growing in volume until alarm belatedly riveted her attention.

Twenty feet farther on, they came abruptly in sight of the furious foaming white of a stream bigger than any they'd yet seen tumbling down a stair step of cliffs. Given the force of the waterfall, even from this distance, the mist wet her face and clung to her eyelashes. Surrounding rocks gleamed with moisture and bright green moss that would make them treacherous.

They wouldn't be crossing here.

Gwen groaned and turned, bumping into Rafe. He stared expressionlessly at the falls. "Pretty."

"I *hate* to backtrack." And that was putting it mildly. She was close to spent and guessed he'd passed that point a couple of hours ago.

Rafe grabbed her arm. "Look."

He didn't sound alarmed, but she still turned her head quickly. *Oh.* A deer accompanied by fawn drank from the stream. They hadn't noticed yet that they weren't alone.

At Gwen's first movement, the deer raised her head, and within moments, both had leaped into the trees.

She and Rafe retreated far enough that the rocks beneath their feet weren't slick, and the roar of the falls wasn't battering their ears.

She'd been taking in their surroundings, desperate for an alternative to making their way downstream far enough for a crossing to be feasible. "If you think you can get up there—" she pointed "—we'd be out of sight."

He looked. His mouth tightened, but he nodded. "Let's do it."

This was…well, a rock climber would have dismissed it as a mere scramble, but for two injured people as tired as they were, it felt more like scaling a straight-up-and-down cliff. A few handholds felt damp from spray blown this far. Her thigh muscles screamed. Once, her foot slipped out of the crack she'd thought secure, and the weight of the pack pulled her backward. Rafe leaned into her, using one strong hand and his bulk to keep her safe until her pulse settled down and she had overcome the rush of adrenaline to try again.

The stiff lower branches of small firs whipped her face but were also strong enough when she seized them to pull herself up.

All the while, a sixth sense she hadn't known she possessed kept her aware of the man behind her. She could *feel* his determination and the sheer will that kept him going. A few muttered curse words escaped him, and a few pained sounds that weren't uttered voluntarily.

I should have had him go ahead of me, she thought, but if she'd done that, she would have fallen far enough that she could have been seriously injured.

More seriously.

If *he* fell…

Gwen blocked that horrifying fear, instead worrying that they'd get up there and find no place adequate to set up even a minimal camp. No, she wouldn't second-guess herself now; from down below, she'd been sure she saw a ledge.

She groped for her next handhold until she satisfied herself that the rock outcrop wouldn't crumble. She heaved herself up another couple of feet. Six inches. A foot. She *had* to be almost there.

And then, suddenly, she was. She was able to crawl forward, brushing aside the dense, low branches of small evergreens. Above her, a bird took indignant flight. All she saw was a flash of yellow. Her pack snagged; she wriggled to free herself. *Keep going, keep going.*

She flopped face down, not sure she could move again. Unless Rafe— No, he stretched out beside her, eyes closed, pale lines of strain on his face.

Neither of them moved for a couple of minutes. Then she sighed, rolled and squirmed to get her arm out of one of the straps of the pack. A hand reached up to help.

"Thanks," she said. Once she was liberated from the pack, she managed to sit up and look around. A rock overhang seemed to promise protection from a helicopter flyover…if they could get to it. More clouds had been gathering, too, the threat of rain another thing she'd refused to let herself dwell on. Neither she nor Rafe had rain gear—or parkas if they should grow chilled once they were wet. This might be the perfect burrow.

She crawled forward, dragging the pack behind her, not caring about the beating her hands were taking. Yes, the ground was reasonably flat right in front of the overhang. They could compress some minor vegetation and be shielded behind the cluster of dark green trees.

"Perfect," she said, and stayed where she was on her hands and knees, swaying.

RAFE DIDN'T THINK he'd hurt like this when he was taking the bullets in the first place. Ten more feet, and he might not have made it.

He wasn't alone. Gwen had hit a wall, too, he saw.

"Hey," he said, "let me give you a hand."

His crawl was like a three-legged race since he knew he'd regret putting any weight on the damaged upper arm. Still, he got far enough to kneel beside her and wrap his good arm around her waist.

"Let yourself go," he murmured.

She collapsed in his hold, but only for a moment. Then she twisted and plopped down on her butt. "Thank you. I was about ready to do a face-plant."

"That actually sounds good."

Resilient enough to laugh, she continued to amaze him.

"I should have given you another shot of morphine at one of our last stops. Why didn't you ask?"

He wasn't about to admit how close he'd come to begging. "Figured the further we could spread them out, the better."

"Actually, that's not really true. Staying on top of the pain helps with recovery."

"I also didn't want to mask any pain that would tell me I was doing more damage," he told her.

"Oh. That makes sense." Apparently making this her first priority, she found what she needed and drew up whatever quantity of the drug she'd calculated for his size. He shifted, unfastened his pants and shoved them down far enough for her to administer the shot in his butt cheek.

And, oh, damn, that felt good. It didn't make him a new man, but it gave him back some of his natural confidence that he could overcome just about any obstacle.

Once she'd capped the used needle and slipped it into a baggy, she said, "We can set up camp here for the night."

Rafe frowned at her as she reached for the

pack again. "You look to me like you need to sit for a minute first."

"I guess there's no hurry. Wait!" She dug almost frantically in her tote, finally coming up with her phone.

Good thought. He all but hung over her shoulder.

No bars. She turned in a circle, lifted it over her head and finally said bitterly, "Things never work when you need them to."

Their lives might depend on them eventually regaining cell phone service, but he didn't have to say a word. She knew.

Less animated, she dropped the phone back into her tote and began searching again. "Let's have a snack before we start setting up."

Rafe couldn't remember how long it had been since they stopped long enough to each eat an energy bar. A single bar hadn't had enough calories for anyone working as hard as they had been, and especially not for someone his size. He pictured a juicy steak and baked potato heaped with sour cream and immediately regretted it when his stomach whined.

After digging deep in the bag, she produced another couple of candy bars. He suspected they'd be running low on those soon—these might even be the last—but he didn't ask. He took one, tore the wrapping and sank his teeth into it—he hadn't even looked to see what it was. It tasted damn good. That's all that mattered. Forget the steak.

"I hope we didn't break branches getting up here," he said after swallowing the last bite.

When she looked at him, he had an unsettling remembrance of thinking how soft the gray of her eyes was. Gentle, comforting. That wasn't true anymore. Maybe not surprising after what they'd gone through, they had darkened, almost seemed haunted. He tried to tell himself he was seeing a reflection of his own feelings about a brutally hard day but suspected that wasn't entirely true.

"Tarp," she said, as if to nudge herself, and opened the pack.

The additional crawling around was manageable for him now after the relief of the painkiller, and he liked the idea of something approaching comfort—and being able to stay put until morning. So he helped set up the tent, push the pad and the single sleeping bag inside it—something to think about later—and tie the green tarp over the too-bright red tent that might as well be a beacon should a helicopter fly right over them.

She set the stove aside and spread out the packets of freeze-dried meals. "Ten."

Rafe gazed at them. "Do you suppose he'd have enjoyed backpacking?"

"Maybe he did it all the time. Still…" She wrinkled her nose. "Weird plan."

"It was, but sure as hell his home office has him down as being on vacation. Heading into the backcountry gave him an excuse to have no cell phone service. In the original plan, the helicopter and my body would have just vanished. No reason to connect him, just one more hiker emerging from the park as far as possible from the crash site."

"Except that he'd flashed his credentials at the hospital and airfield."

"Those couldn't have been his."

"Bill knew his real name." She told him her speculation about the pair meeting in the past and said, "If that was so, it must have come as a shock to Kimball."

"That's one way to put it," Rafe said dryly.

"Do you suppose once he hiked to a trailhead, he was going to call someone for a lift?"

Instinct had Rafe shaking his head. "I doubt it. I'll bet he'd have put out his thumb. Some vacationers or other backpackers would have picked him up. A night at a hotel at SeaTac, and he could have flown out."

She sniffed. "*I* wouldn't have picked him up. Or I'd have kicked him out of my car ten miles down the road. Unless he managed a personality upgrade."

Rafe grinned. "Well, he wouldn't be threatening to shoot whoever gave him a ride."

"I don't know." She looked contemplative. "He jumped straight to hostile the minute he set eyes on me. He didn't even know who I was, and he was bristling. It was like his default. You know?" She shook her head. "I'd have been less suspicious if he'd dialed it back a little and tried a semipleasant 'Hey, this area is restricted. Are you looking for somebody?'"

Rafe cast his mind back, trying to remember why he'd instinctively disliked a fellow agent he'd never had much to do with. It wasn't the first time someone rubbed him wrong, of course. The snap judgments he made about people were presumably based on a subconscious conclusion rather than conscious reasoning. Because he and Kimball hadn't been assigned to work together, he'd had no reason to dwell on that twinge of dislike.

Now, though, he said, "I think that's what I responded to, also. Put a bunch of federal agents together for the first time, and there's often some posturing. Who's the alpha here? But we don't fight to determine it. We work together, smooth out any rough spots, determine strengths and weaknesses, and depend on each other. Kimball had a bad attitude. I saw him bump another guy's shoulder hard in passing when really he was the one who should have stepped aside. I didn't like the way he looked at a particular female agent, either."

"So, your dislike was more rational than you knew."

"I guess so." The corner of his mouth quirked. "On the job, I sometimes have to go with my gut. There are times I need to walk back my opinion, but not often."

She sighed. "This time, you were right on target."

"Except being arrogant doesn't translate to being willing to violate the very principles you're supposed to be defending."

"No." She slipped on a fleece jacket and zipped it. "Do you think it would be safe to take a quick nap before we make dinner?"

"I don't think anyone can sneak up on us here. We'll have to get cozy, though."

Her gaze shied from his. "Not like we have a lot of choice."

Was she still holding on to any doubt that he was who he claimed to be? He said carefully, "I'm afraid not."

The smile she offered him was more complicated than it appeared on the surface but was still so beautiful he quit breathing.

"I'd be delighted," she told him.

What?

Oh, getting cozy. Somehow, he doubted either of them would stay conscious long enough for the proximity to get awkward.

She let him make his awkward way into the tent first before following him. She wadded up extra clothing for pillows, and then they settled down side by side on top of the sleeping bag. Despite the talk of cuddling, their bodies barely brushed each other. He didn't like the distance between them. He wanted to roll onto his side and gather her into his arms, but he knew better. Any more intimacy than absolutely necessary had to be her decision.

Scaring her was the absolute last thing he wanted to do.

Chapter Eight

Gwen lay completely still until she was sure Rafe had fallen asleep. As his breathing deepened, genuine relaxation replaced what she'd recognized as pretend calm. A nerve in his cheek jerked a couple of times; his fingers twitched. He had to be dreaming.

Only then did she give herself permission to roll onto her side facing away from him, close her eyes and surrender to her own tiredness.

As it turned out, for all its aches and pains, her body was ready to let go, but her brain kept working. She didn't understand why she had been so determined not to be the first to fall asleep.

The answer just leaped into her mind: *I'd have been too vulnerable. Was I afraid he might hurt me?* she wondered in shock, but that wasn't right. Mostly…she didn't really *know* him, she realized. They'd gone through an awful lot today, but none of it allowed much in the way of conversation. So it was true that, in many respects, Rafe Salazar remained a stranger.

Not entirely, though. Despite suffering from extreme pain, he'd reached out over and over to save her from falls, to support her.

Yes, she reminded herself, but just because Kimball turned out to be corrupt didn't mean Rafe wasn't conning her. He could really and truly have been under arrest; only whoever he and Kimball were both working for had determined to shut him up before he could be compelled to speak to law enforcement. Snatch him before he was fully conscious and be sure he never had a chance to open his mouth. The drug trade was notoriously violent. Mistakes—like getting arrested—she knew could be punishable by death.

Yet her instincts insisted that Rafe was one of the good guys. He could so easily have overpowered her, taken the pack, the food and the morphine, and gone on the run by himself.

Yes. Instead, he'd been…careful with her. Gentle. *She* mattered.

She had a sinking feeling that some of the tension came from her awareness of him as a man. And…maybe some reciprocal awareness on his part?

Face it, he was a beautiful man. She resisted the temptation to roll over to study him. She didn't have to; behind closed eyes, she saw him. Big, broad-shouldered, lean and muscled. With those cheekbones and penetrating dark eyes, he could have modeled, although she felt sure he would laugh at the idea.

So, okay, if she'd met him another way, she'd have been interested. As it was…

A flutter of panic explained some of her self-consciousness. It would be easy to fall for him, given their mutual dependence. If she was okay with a casual easy-come-easy-go relationship, that wouldn't be any big deal. But she never had been. Having the last guy she'd been involved with ditch her the way he did left scars on top of her natural caution. Anyway, if—when—she and Rafe came upon other people or were finally able to make a call and get rescued, they'd go their own ways. His life was really complicated, and from what he'd said, he didn't even work out of the Seattle office, assuming the DEA had one.

Better to be sensible now.

Smart conclusion.

And, face it, the mutual attraction thing could be entirely wishful thinking. He might be protecting her because he needed her to get him out of a wilderness he couldn't navigate on his own.

Fine, she thought.

Having figured out what made her skittish, she was armored now. With that settled, she sank into sleep with astonishing speed.

THE NEXT THING she knew, she woke up with a jolt. Had she heard something alarming? The helicopter, or—

A hand smoothed hair back from her forehead. Rafe, of course. *Oh, heavens!* Somehow she'd ended up with her head on his upper arm, his body spooning hers.

Subconscious? Weren't you listening?

Apparently not.

"Sorry," he murmured. "I need to get up."

He needed to— *Oh.* Now that she thought about it, she did, too.

Busy with her thoughts, she let Rafe maneuver out the unzipped opening, climb to his feet and head for a rock outcrop. Once he was mostly out of sight, she tensed her stomach muscles in preparation for standing up herself and grimaced. Now that she thought about it, *everything* hurt. Darn it. She stayed in decent physical shape! She did.

Apparently, her several-mile three-times-a-week jog really wasn't enough. And then there were her ribs.

Glad Rafe couldn't see her as she managed to scoot out of the tent and get up without a hint of grace, Gwen went the opposite direction from him. Her thighs were *really* unhappy with her when she squatted.

Surely, she'd feel better in the morning. She sighed and made her way back to their encampment.

Dusk deepened the sky to violet tinged with a darker purple that was almost…gray. Clouds, she realized. It was good he'd woken up. A threat of rain looked more realistic, which made her glad they'd set up the tent.

She returned to find Rafe studying the tent with what she read as disfavor. She knew why. "Do you suppose that's his favorite color?"

Rafe grunted. "I'm thinking he chose it to grab attention. If he was lucky, he'd be seen half a dozen times by other hikers who could testify that he was by himself, just a lone, innocent backpacker."

Thank heavens for the green tarp. She'd succeeded in stretching it out above and in front of the tent, tying cords to branches and, in one case, a rock, giving them some room to sit in front without getting wet if it rained. Without asking her, Rafe now took the jackknife from a pocket in the pack and set to cutting branches that he laid over the tarp and sides of the tent.

"Looks like a deer blind," he said, closing the knife. "A lot of work for one night, but worth it if that damn helicopter flies overhead come morning."

"I've been thinking about that," she said.

In the dimming light, she could no longer make out his face clearly but could tell he'd narrowed his eyes. "Am I going to like this?"

"I don't know." She hesitated. "It's just…this was a really hard day."

"I can't argue." He rolled his one good shoulder and, with obvious effort, lowered himself to the ground again.

"Well… I'm wondering if it might be a good idea to stay here tomorrow and not set out again until the following morning. Right now, we're staggering around blind. I suspect that given an extra twenty-four hours, you'd do a lot of healing."

"I might, but then they could get ahead of us. That's not a comfortable idea."

HE'D HATED TO remind her of a brutal truth but knew he had to. That might be a small shudder she tried to hide.

After a minute, she said quietly, "You're right."

End of conversation. Gwen fired up the stove, and they agreed on an entrée from the array of freeze-dried meals Kimball had chosen. She set aside two of the packets. The guy was—

had obviously been—a meat eater. Which made Rafe think.

"What kind of predators do we need to watch out for?" he asked.

"You mean, aside from the human ones?"

At her wry tone, he grimaced. "Just thought I should know about any other threats."

She stirred the concoction that smelled better than it looked. "The only two animals in the park that can be a danger to people are black bears, and usually only females with cubs near, and cougars, which we're unlikely to see. Once in a while, a cougar will attack a human, but it's not common. There are smaller predators, like bobcats, which are rare to spot, and, hey, there was an episode a few years back when a mountain goat over in the Olympic Mountains attacked a backpacker. Most often, when people are injured by wildlife in one of the parks, it's not the animal's fault. It's because the humans have forgotten all common sense, if they ever had any. People will go so far as to set their kid on the back of a bear so they can get an exciting photo."

"I've heard stories like that. I'd say they get what they have coming, except it's their children who might suffer."

"Yes. There's a reason the park service has worked so hard to keep bears away from both roads and campgrounds in the parks. Yellowstone was most notorious for problems way back when. You wouldn't think you'd have to tell tourists that a moose is a really big animal with an impressive rack on his head, and you might want to give him space."

"Are there moose here at Rainier?"

"No, but there are elk and foxes, not to mention marmots and picas, as well as rabbits, deer mice and—" she pointed upward "—bats."

The darting motion against the dusk sky was familiar.

She dished up his share of the stew in a light-weight bowl and ate hers out of the pan. The ranger-type patter had cut down on the tension, at least on his side. This was the first time since Eaton opened the front door upon seeing a familiar face and gunfire raked the small rambler that Rafe had felt relaxed. He couldn't remember what time that happened. Yesterday, for sure. Twenty-four hours ago? He wouldn't have survived most of the ensuing day if not for Gwen. Watching surreptitiously, he decided she had relaxed, too. Tension was less apparent on her face. He'd say they had been lucky to find someplace as safe as this, but luck hadn't had anything to do with it. He could thank her for that, too.

"Coffee?" she asked. "We even have sugar and powdered creamer, if you take either."

He moved from side to side to scratch his back against the rough rock he leaned against. "All the pleasures of home. Coffee sounds good. Yes to both."

She chuckled. "You're not one of those tough guys who drinks his coffee black even if it tastes like battery acid?"

He let himself smile, too. "Not me."

She heated some water, washed the dinner dishes with soap and a sponge she'd found in the pack, then started over with water for the coffee. He should be helping, but one-handed, how useful would he be, anyway?

"You know how to handle a gun," he commented. "You're a good shot, too. How'd you learn?"

Watching the small pan as if her focused concentration would make the water boil faster, she said, "I...knew someone." She paused. "Oh, I guess it doesn't matter. A foster father. Kind of paranoid. You know, the kind who was sure the government would be coming for his guns. I guess he must not have expressed much of that thinking to social workers, or his foster care license might have been suspended, but anyway. He taught all of us kids how to handle a .22 rifle and both an old-fashioned Colt six-shooter and a semiautomatic. It was fun shooting cans off a fence rail. It probably goes without saying that I didn't hurry out to buy my own handgun once I was living alone. In fact, I haven't handled one since I was in that foster home. He really drilled us, though. I guess some things you don't forget."

"Like riding a bike." If a little more lethal.

She shrugged, then concentrated on pouring not-quite-boiling water into a metal cup and some other container she'd unearthed from the kitchen supplies. "I never thought I'd be thankful for the skill."

"No," he said gently. "Maybe once you're home, you should drop him a note." He added half a spoonful of creamer to the coffee, followed by part of a paper packet of sugar.

Her smile looked sad. "Maybe I should. I didn't make any effort to stay in touch, and I feel bad about that."

Rafe guessed that she'd as soon drop this whole subject, but it would probably be at least a couple of hours before they'd crawl into the tent again, this time for the night. They had to talk about something. She'd gotten him curious earlier anyway, when he'd asked what had motivated her to become a medical first responder. There'd been something in her expression…

Trying to sound easy, undemanding, he asked, "What happened to your parents?"

With a hint of belligerence, she retorted, "Why don't you tell me about *your* parents?"

"Fair enough." His background was more complicated than this answer would tell her, but he could answer the question without getting personal. "Believe it or not, they're both university professors. Philosophy for Dad—I learned early on to tune him out when he got off on his thing—and Mom is a linguist. Teaches several languages at the university level and is working on a grammar and vocabulary dictionary for an obscure African language on the verge of disappearing. This is following work on a Central American Indigenous language."

"Huh."

Rafe laughed. "They're smart people. Well-meaning parents, but heads in the clouds. Mom would be away for months at a time on one of her research trips. Dad has written several books. I could tell you the titles, but they wouldn't mean any more to you than they did to me."

"That…doesn't sound like an easy household to grow up in."

Not for the first time, Rafe had that feeling she was seeing deeper than he liked. She'd hit the nail on the head.

"Your turn," he said roughly.

She watched him for another minute or two, then nodded. "Dad died when I was a kid, too young to remember him. One of those heart things that no one predicts. He was in his twenties, playing in a pickup basketball game, and just collapsed. Gone."

But she hadn't aimed to be a cardiologist, he thought.

"Mom…" Gwen had a gift for stillness, but now she shifted in a way that gave away her discomfort. "She and I were in a car accident. Head-on, drunk driver. The car was pushed through a guardrail and over something like a thirty-foot drop. This makes me really obvious, doesn't it? Mom was killed right away. I was…in bad shape. I thought I was going to die, too. I guess emergency response was reasonably quick. It felt like forever, but it probably always does when you're trapped like I was. I was eleven and in the front seat, too. The car was crumpled, and they couldn't get mom *or* me out, which was bad because she was *right there* and so obviously dead, and my legs were broken and I was bleeding bad. They used crowbars and whatever else they could lay their hands on, because later, they told me they didn't think I'd have survived a long wait."

He swore softly.

"They were calm, even when they probably

weren't really, and caring. This guy got an IV line in me, gave me oxygen when he thought I needed it and stayed with me except when the others made him get out of the way. He just talked, even told a few jokes, and he held my hand."

She wasn't crying at the memory, just appeared pensive. "So. Like I said, I'm not subtle. I wanted to grow up to do what he did."

He should have expected something like this, but hadn't. He felt fierce anger and a tight knot of pain behind the different kind of pain in his breastbone, but knew he shouldn't let her know what a hit he'd taken on her behalf.

"So, did they give you the good stuff, too?"

Obviously startled, Gwen giggled. "Yes, they did. Whatever they put in that IV was amazing."

"Morphine?"

"Who knows?"

Rafe set down his cup. "Did you ever see that guy again?"

"Yes. He visited me a couple of times in the hospital and, way later, got permission for me to ride along in his ambulance a couple of times. I wished…" This shrug was a cloaking device.

"Wished?"

"He could have taken me as a foster kid. I knew better than to ask, and he didn't offer."

"If he was single, he probably wouldn't have been allowed to take in a girl."

"That's true." Her chin rose, and she wiped the memories and regrets from her expression. "There are a few candy bars left. Do you want one?"

"I don't think I can resist," he admitted. "The only thing is, we may not be able to share a tent if neither of us can brush our teeth."

Gwen laughed. "Who gets to stay out in the rain?"

He grinned. "I'm the patient. Gives me priority, right?"

"You wish." She laughed again. "We're really going to owe that creep Kimball, you know. As it happens, I noticed a handy-dandy little travel pack with toothpaste. And get this, it looks like it came with two toothbrushes! Sort of miniature ones, and maybe meant to be disposable, but they'll do us."

"Has he used either?" Rafe asked dubiously. He wouldn't mind sharing spit with some people, but Bruce Kimball wasn't one of those.

"I doubt it. Doesn't look like anything has been touched since he packed it."

The silence that fell after that felt surprisingly easy. They'd said quite a bit for two people who had known each other for only twelve hours or so. He was glad for the fleece as the temperature dropped. Night sounds he wouldn't have otherwise noticed were soothing in their own way: a few hoots that had to be from an owl, or two of them chatting, small squeaks and rustles, the very distant murmur that he guessed was the muted roar of the waterfall. Once, there was a sharp squeal, quickly cut off, and Rafe reminded himself that owls were hunters.

Finally, he said, "We have a plan for tomorrow?"

Gwen sighed. "I wish."

He waited, and after a minute she went on.

"If possible, I'd like to reach the top of this ridge. It would help a lot to get a glimpse of the mountain."

That made sense.

"My goal has been to reach a trail, both for easier walking and in hopes we'll encounter other people. But I've had second thoughts."

He'd vaguely had the same hope, but now that the subject was out in the open, he had concerns, too.

"Would the people after us hesitate to gun down a couple of backpackers that happen by?" she asked.

Rafe suspected she knew the answer as well as he did.

"I doubt it," he said harshly. "Also, if we can move faster on a trail, so can they."

"So…maybe we could sort of make our way a few hundred yards from the trail. If we're lucky, we might spot a ranger. I'm pretty sure most of them are armed these days, and I assume they carry a radio with some distance."

Rafe didn't wonder aloud what the odds were of happening on a park ranger, partly because her plan was as good as any.

And *that* was assuming they kept ahead of their pursuers long enough to stumble upon a trail.

Chapter Nine

There had been an odd sense of intimacy while they talked, Gwen couldn't help thinking. She'd told Rafe things she hadn't talked about in a very long time, if ever. None of her relationships with men had progressed to the point where she wanted to tell them about the eon she'd spent trapped in the crumpled metal of the car along with her dead mother. Doing so made her feel...vulnerable.

Damn it, there was that word again.

Especially since, now that she thought of it, *he* hadn't shared anything comparable in *his* background. His parents were college professors. So, why wasn't he an academic, too? If there'd been a hint, it must have to do with the suggestion that neither parent was all that present for their son— or for their other children, if he had siblings.

That car accident had been what a psychologist would call a defining experience for her, and she guessed he'd had one of his own. But really, he didn't owe her answers. The bigger question was why *she'd* felt compelled to tell him something so important about herself.

Something he might have found mildly interesting, Gwen reminded herself. It wasn't a deep, dark secret. And they didn't have a real relationship.

Well, not the kind she'd been thinking about, anyway.

After their last depressing exchange, silence settled again until she stirred.

"Let me give you another shot, just enough to give you a chance to sleep, and then we should get ready for bed. An early departure might be a good idea."

"I agree." Was he frowning? "I can do without the morphine."

"No, you can't. Keep on top of the pain, remember? The better you sleep, the more relaxed your muscles, the more healing will happen."

He muttered under his breath but didn't argue while she found the supplies in her tote bag. As she drew up an accurate dose, he held the flashlight, shading the beam with his hand to limit how far out it could be seen from. While he had it on, they put toothpaste on the brushes, and she wet a washcloth and grabbed the bar of soap from Kimball's well-stocked pack. She had to have sweated more today than she usually did in a week.

Rafe eyed the washcloth and said, "Do I get kicked out of the tent if I don't follow your example?"

She made a face at him. "You're a patient. I'm assuming you started the day spotlessly clean."

"I'll bet you did, too."

"We'll see how you feel tomorrow." She waved the syringe. "Drop those drawers."

She enjoyed hearing him laugh, suspecting that the brief sting was worth the rush of euphoria and relief. He pulled the trousers back up, rising to his feet as she collected her toiletry supplies and sought privacy to do some minimal scrubbing. He presumably stepped a few feet away from their small camp to use the facilities, but she didn't hear a thing. When she returned to the tent, he had half sat on a rock and was wrestling off the boots.

"Oh! I can help—"

"Got 'em." He pulled off the socks, too, seemed to glance at her, and removed his pants and the Polartec quarter-zip, leaving him wearing only a pair of stretch boxers he'd appropriated—although he hadn't looked happy about it—and a T-shirt.

He was right, Gwen realized. He had only a single change of clothes in the pack, and she was in even worse shape. If only she'd been able to grab her suitcase! As it was, she could wear the Nomex suit one day instead of her current clothes, but it wasn't ideal for scrambling through the woods and over rocky ridges, to put it mildly. Given their extremely limited wardrobes, they needed to mostly strip at night. She would definitely do that stripping in the pitch dark, preferably once he'd already gone into the tent.

As if he wouldn't be able to tell how little she was wearing the minute she slipped into that sleeping bag with him.

Rafe suggested he get in the sleeping bag first, which was logical. They'd laid it out so their heads would be close to the tent flap in case of trouble. He held the flashlight, a bare glimmer escaping the top of the sleeping bag. Enough to guide her. Gwen wanted to claim she wasn't sleepy yet, but it wasn't true, even after the nap. Anyway, what would she do? Despite the matches Kimball had packed, they hadn't dared light a fire she could sit beside.

Just do it.

She crouched, mostly lay down and squirmed like a snake until she was far enough in. Of course, she bumped and slid against him the whole way. She tried very hard to pretend the solid wall that gave off such welcoming heat wasn't a man she'd known only a day.

Rafe only said, "You can use me as a pillow," and then, "No rain yet."

"No." Where else could she put her head? She should have bundled up some of their limited clothing again to form a facsimile of a cushion, at least for him.

She lay rigid until she felt light-headed and became aware she'd been holding her breath.

"Don't be afraid of me," he murmured, his mouth brushing her hair.

"I...don't think I am," she said after a minute. "It's just... I'm not used to hopping into bed with a guy I don't know that well." And that was putting it mildly.

Humor in his voice, he said, "We've had quite a first date, though, wouldn't you say?"

The laugh was just what she needed. "It's definitely the most eventful I've ever been on."

He chuckled, too, and she felt his chest vibrate even though she wasn't touching it. Was she?

"Want me to tell some jokes?"

"Jokes?" Then she got it. "Like the paramedic. Thank you, but no. Unless you have a really great one."

He told her a bawdy one that had her laughing despite herself. After that, when he said, "Can we get more comfortable?" and eased his arm beneath her head to wrap her in an embrace, she was relaxed enough to allow it. Even rest her head where she could hear his heartbeat and have some wistful thoughts she wouldn't let herself put into words.

Too concrete for something that wasn't happening.

IT WOULD BE nice if they could have shut down and *stayed* shut down until the dawn light beckoned them with a promise of a less painful day, but the truth was, Rafe thought he and Gwen both slept pretty well for three or four hours, but after that, he, for one, hurt and couldn't stay still, she had a nightmare and flailed an arm at his face, and, unable to help waking each other up, they tried half a dozen positions that didn't remain comfortable for more than an hour.

He took pleasure in holding her close for a few minutes at a time, wishing he had the right to cup her breast or slide his hand over her lithe, subtly curvaceous body. Those moments were torturous in their own way and didn't last long.

By morning, his mood was testy, and his first glimpse of Gwen's face suggested she was as tired and grumpy as he was. He submitted to another shot, at which his muscles untangled as if he'd had a deep-tissue massage. *Thank God.*

"You sure you don't want one, too?" he asked,

nodding at the syringe she was dropping into a plastic bag seemingly made for the purpose.

She grimaced. "I wish."

A cup of coffee and a couple of handfuls of trail mix helped both of them.

"That wasn't as cozy as I hoped it would be," she said after a lengthy silence.

Rafe was startled into laughing and was glad to see the corners of her mouth twitch. "You're right. It was more like a high school wrestling match."

She giggled. "I don't think I've ever really slept with anyone."

That was interesting. He said, "I haven't often, and on those occasions, we shared at least a queen-size bed. Not the same thing."

"No." Gwen sighed. "It's infuriating when you want to toss and turn, but you're too trussed up to be able even to turn over."

He lifted an eyebrow. "And you wondered why I was so desperate for you to release me from that damn backboard."

"Oh. Yes." She actually looked apologetic. "I'm sorry."

Rafe smiled. "Don't be. We had a lot going on at the time."

"Yes." Her shoulders slumped. "I suppose we should pack up."

"Yeah," he said gruffly.

Without another word, she started on the cords holding up the tarp, then rolled it, the sleeping bag and pad, and broke down the tent. He was able to take the stove apart and pack up what little they'd left out.

He watched as she delved in her fat tote bag and started discarding things. He saw her hesitate before putting an electronic reader back, but she chose to abandon a swirled glass paperweight about the side of a baseball—a gift from her friend, she said, after glancing at him— along with a box of tampons he pretended not to notice, a bottle of hand lotion, a zip bag that he suspected held makeup and a bag with a couple of wrapped presents she'd been taking back to friends. She looked sad about those, but he didn't say anything, because she was right: the lighter their load, the faster they could move.

She ditched most of the contents of what she called a trauma bag. "If one of us gets hurt again…" she mumbled. "But what are the odds we'll need any of this stuff?" That included emergency airway supplies, something she called a pleural decompression kit, IV supplies and blood pressure cuffs. The bulk and weight saved was substantial. About all she held on to were packages of bandaging materials, which she shifted back into the pack.

While they were able to weed out a couple

of things from Kimball's pack, most of what it held was necessary. As in lifesaving. Rafe hesitated over an extra magazine for Kimball's semiautomatic, briefly bouncing it in his hand, but made the decision to keep it.

Lifesaving.

As he attached the tent, sleeping bag and pad to the pack, Gwen asked how he felt today.

If he'd been honest, he'd have said, *Worse than yesterday.* Wasn't that always the case with injuries and abused muscles? Of course, he shrugged and said, "Better."

Gwen rolled her eyes. "Good for you. *I'm* sore."

"Walk it off."

She stuck her tongue out at him, which he fully deserved. Walking wasn't in their immediate future. Scrambling, climbing, bushwhacking was more like it.

And so it proved. They went up instead of back down, Rafe glad she went first so she couldn't see his gritted teeth or hear his mumbled curses as his thigh and hip especially cramped and zinged with electrical impulses and occasionally felt as if a knife was stabbing him. And this was *after* a dose of morphine. He'd been injured enough times to know he could have forced himself to go on no matter what, but he didn't want to contemplate how bad this trek would have been without the medical aid.

The terrain was incredibly difficult, heavily forested yet steep and rocky. Most of the time, they couldn't see more than ten paces away, but at least they had the comfort of knowing no one else could see them, either.

They obviously scared what wildlife they spotted. Birds went silent long before the humans reached them, then took startled wing at the last moment, often in bright flashes seen out of the corner of his eye. Rafe continued to hear running water, whether the same stream or different ones, he didn't know.

They didn't talk. The effort of climbing coupled with their various disabilities and the muscle soreness left from yesterday's exertions meant that he, at least, had to concentrate to take each painful step. To use a branch to heave himself upward. Not that he'd have gone far if he did fall; he'd just slam into a tree trunk. The thought made him wince. If he took a solid blow on his thigh or already excruciating rib cage...

Don't think about it.

When he saw daylight ahead, he clenched his jaw, unwilling to groan with relief. He kept up a facade of strength with everyone. Hell, maybe even to himself. By the time he'd been a teenager, he'd perfected the swagger, the confidence, the incredulity if anyone was foolish enough to challenge *him*.

The tree line ended suddenly, exposing rough-textured gray granite. By the time they'd scrambled the rest of the way to what he prayed was the ridgetop, he'd scraped and nicked his hands in several places.

In the back of his mind was the realization that he might have left a blood trail to follow, but really, what were the odds their pursuers would climb so exactly behind them? And, no, as he straightened cautiously, he saw that neither hand bled copiously. Just smears.

Gwen grabbed his arm. "Look!"

He took in a stunning vista. Way the hell down from them were at least a couple of lakes. And when he turned his head slightly, there was the mountain, enormous almost past understanding. Flying by it didn't count as a view. A few clouds drifted around the gleaming summit. It occurred to him that they were quite a long way from Mount Rainier here, but seeing the landscape formed by its historic eruptions made him a little queasy.

"Wouldn't want to be here if Rainier suddenly decided to blow its top," he remarked.

"No." Gwen paused. "All the Northwest volcanoes are monitored for seismic activity. Scientists learned from the Mount Saint Helens's eruption and at least delude themselves they can give some warning."

"Uh-huh." He bet the most magnificent mountain he'd ever seen knew how to keep its secrets. "Can we sit?" he added.

"Oh! Yes, of course." She joined him in looking around, then pointed. "That looks good."

"Good" would have been a recliner made for a large man, one that allowed him to put his feet up, but his mouth twitched into a smile at the thought. Somebody was getting soft.

The rock was flat enough to let him plant his butt. Gwen sat close to him, keeping her arms at her sides as if she didn't want to brush him. That bothered him, given how snug that sleeping bag had been, but he had to respect her need to maintain some space.

Both allowed themselves a few quiet, contemplative minutes before she dug out the water bottle and bags of peanuts and raisins.

"It's…steep going forward," he said finally.

"Yes."

More open than was safe, too, although following the ridge would be worse.

"Do you recognize where we are?"

"I think I might. Let me get the map out." She set down her bag of peanuts and dug deeper in the pack. "Oh, and my phone, too! Maybe we're high enough…"

She got nothing. They both stared at the black screen.

"You didn't turn it off so the battery wouldn't run down?"

She looked stricken. "It never occurred to me. I hardly ever do."

It took him a minute to ask calmly, "When did you last charge it?"

"Um…early evening before we left. And—" she shifted a little "—the battery isn't what it used to be."

"I should have said something." Why hadn't he? He upgraded phones often to have maximum battery life even more than the features touted in commercials.

"Why didn't your boss give you yours back?" she asked, sounding timid.

"I didn't have it on me when I was shot. In the chaos, who knows what happened to it? The shooter might even have grabbed it, thinking he could get in and see who I'd been talking to."

Gwen nodded. She didn't want to meet his eyes, he thought. He refused to let her feel as if she'd screwed up, not when she'd been his lifesaver in so many ways.

"You thought you'd be home in a few hours when you got on that helicopter," he pointed out. "Unless you usually turn it off when you're in the air, you had no reason to give it a thought."

"Not then," she argued. "But after—" *After I shot and killed a man*, was what she meant.

Her fingers curled around the phone so tightly her knuckles showed white. Rafe pried it out of her hand and took that hand in his.

"Remember how busy we were? I was with you when you checked for bars. I should have thought of it, as well. I'm the guy who does this for a living, after all."

She gave a watery-sounding chuckle, even though there wasn't a tear to be seen. "Better you than me."

"I sit behind a desk sometimes."

The chuckle became a laugh, and he realized he was smiling, too. Either the morphine was speaking or the ever-present pain, but he felt incredibly reluctant to move. *Yeehaw*, he thought, remembering his gung-ho self from a decade ago. *Maybe I'm too old for this.*

Something to think about later.

She did say, "We had a portable charger in the helicopter. We always do. Only…" No need to finish that sentence. She could only grab so much so fast.

After a minute, Gwen tipped her head sideways to rest it on his upper arm for a moment, whether in understanding, solidarity or apology, he didn't know. He turned his head enough to brush a kiss against her forehead.

Then they both retreated as if they'd never shared that moment and resumed crunching on their lunch.

Until he felt a subliminal tingle right before Gwen stiffened, hearing as he did the distant sound of a helicopter.

"Oh, no!"

Could be a park ranger helicopter or a search and rescue one, he tried to tell himself, but his mouth twisted. When had he last been that optimistic?

No. They had to get out of sight and fast.

Chapter Ten

Why, oh, why had they had let themselves stop out in the open without first identifying a way to get out of sight quickly? That had been Gwen's cardinal rule so far.

Frantically, she spun to look around. The drop forward off the ridge was too precipitous for them. They had to go one way or the other...or back the way they'd come to get under the cover of the forest.

"Back!" Rafe said, grabbing the pack and slinging it over his shoulder before she could protest.

Maybe she'd been carrying the pack too long, because she felt unbalanced enough that she stumbled almost immediately and went to her knees.

Rafe yanked her up. She clutched the tote bag and scuttled after him over the rough ground.

The distinctive roar of a helicopter grew nearer. Given her experience, it should be a good sound, even heartwarming. They were on their way to save lives. Or on the ground, hearing backup coming. Her current fear made clear how drastically her perspective had changed.

They held hands as they skidded over the back edge of the ridge. The trees seemed impossibly far away. The climb hadn't been *that* long, had it? How could they possibly make it before the shadow of the bird covered them?

Rafe pulled her sideways. Her ankle tried to give way, but he wouldn't let her fall. Through the salt of sweat dripping into her eyes, Gwen saw what he aimed for. Not an overhang as perfect as they'd found the first day, but a jumble of slabs that might provide cover.

She still couldn't see the approaching helicopter, but it could be upon them any second, and someone in it would be using high-powered binoculars to search for movement or colors that didn't fit.

They'd draped the tarp over the pack, but it was subtly too bright, and they weren't currently surrounded by greenery, anyway.

The next time she stumbled, it was because Rafe had bent over and was pulling her between broken slabs.

"Get down!" he ordered. "Go, go!"

There was a narrow passage barely open to the sky above. He shoved her ahead of him, then pushed the pack after her. Somehow, he had lowered himself to a crouch that had to be unbearably painful, and he had his gun in his hands. The hard look on his face scared her as much as the circumstances.

The roar had become deafening. She squeezed against gritty rock, feeling the print of it on her cheek, trying to make it absorb her.

The shadow did literally fall over them, giving her chills.

But, oh God, oh God, it was continuing on. The terrible sound receded.

Rafe lowered his hands so his weapon pointed at the ground in front of his feet. "It might circle back," he said tensely.

"I never saw it. Did you?"

"A glimpse." With dark humor, he added, "Good thing Kimball didn't extend his passion for red to this fleece top."

"I never studied the map," she said, trying to sound as calm as Rafe did. This wasn't an ideal place to lay it out.

"No hurry," he said.

She kept leaning, not sure she'd still be on her feet if it weren't for the rock. Except that she felt sure if she started to topple, Rafe would step in to support her. The very thought made her ashamed. He was in worse shape than she was. He was her *patient*.

Only they'd moved irrevocably past that, hadn't they?

He swiveled to look right at her, his eyes even darker than usual, penetrating. "You're not going to like this." His voice was gritty. "It occurs to me that nobody but Bill and Kimball knew about you. I'm…not going to tell you to take off on your own right away. You could get into trouble, and I'd never know."

"You need me."

He bent his head in agreement. "But if they see me but not you, I want you to hide. Run. Whatever you can do." His jaw muscles flexed. "Seeing you die for me—"

"I feel the same about you!" she cried.

"But they'd leave you behind, not knowing what you've seen. They will never leave me."

"Rafe." She was afraid it came out as a whimper. He leaned toward her…just before they both heard the hum growing in volume.

He said a few vicious words and squeezed his eyes closed.

Gwen tried even harder to become one with the rock.

If they miraculously found a trail, he'd make her leave him, Rafe decided. Who would know she was anything but another hiker trying to complete the Wonderland Trail, which circled all the way around Mount Rainier? She'd go for it if he convinced her that she could safely find help and send them back for him.

Nice, selfless thought, except he hadn't seen any suggestion of a trail as he scanned the vista, and he was pretty sure Gwen hadn't, either. Thinking about how close she'd come to falling yesterday, he knew he couldn't send her on alone. She didn't deserve any of what had happened to her in the past day and a half, and he was determined to protect her from anything more.

Yeah, except exhaustion, stress and the fun of being hunted by killers. Of perpetually feeling eyes on their backs and looking down from above.

Maybe the feet-on-the-ground hunters had gone in entirely different directions. Given the vast wilderness, it was possible, even likely. Rafe just couldn't count on it.

The fact that the helicopter had flown up one side of the ridge and back on the other gave him a bad feeling. He thought he'd have heard the roar, however muted, if it had been flying the kind of pattern they'd seen before. Had it come so close today out of sheer logic or because one of the pursuers had set eyes on them or just spotted a few broken branches or scuffs in the loamy soil beneath the trees?

"Okay," he said finally. "I think we can assume the search has shifted to another area. Let's move while we can."

He was very aware of her swallow followed by her squaring her shoulders. Gutsy as always.

"You're right. First, though, if we can get in a slightly more open spot, I want to take a look at the map again."

Rafe nodded, grabbed the straps of the pack and pulled it behind him as he edged out of their temporary refuge. Gwen came right behind, carrying the tote bag he'd started to equate with Mary Poppins's bag. Gwen had stuffed some damn wonderful things in it.

The minute there was room, she spread the map and pointed at the trio of lakes she thought they were looking down on. No trail came near, of course, but he didn't see any good alternative but to drop down to them, then make a torturous way south toward what the map had labeled as the Northern Loop Trail.

He didn't bother commenting. Gwen folded the map and stowed it at the top of the pack before closing it.

"You still carrying the gun?" Rafe asked.

She nodded.

"Safety on?"

"Yes." She turned her back to him and lifted the layers of tops she wore. "You can check it if you want."

He wanted to. The idea of her taking a tumble and the damn gun going off and potentially putting a bullet in her was enough to give him nightmares.

The safety was still in the off position, which didn't entirely satisfy him, but what could he say? Conceivably, they might find themselves under fire and need to respond without delay.

She hefted the pack again, something else Rafe didn't like, but he slung the now lighter tote bag over his shoulder and let her go ahead.

The next hours were grueling. Tree cover was sporadic, rocks crumbling, drop-offs potential killers. The sun climbed high in the sky, then began to descend. Rafe hadn't seen anyplace flat enough to set up the tent or even where they could lie side by side. They had to go on. Scrambling downward put more stress on his quads than going up had. His thigh had passed sheer agony and had almost become numb. A couple of times, he thumped it with a fist to be sure he still had any feeling in it.

They took a few breaks, which weren't much help. Looking at Gwen disturbed him. She'd lost enough weight to be visible, which shouldn't be possible in a day and a half. Her cheekbones stood out more prominently, and her eyes had sunken deeper in her face. He wanted to believe he was imagining things, but couldn't quite do so. She studied him the way he did her, but he didn't ask if he looked as bad as she did.

His gaze rested on her feet in the athletic shoes. *Good tread*, he thought, not for the first time, but no protection for her ankles if one twisted.

He clung to the idea of setting up camp on the shore of one of those pretty, probably rarely visited lakes, although at the moment, he couldn't see any of them.

Disaster struck between one heartbeat and the next. Ahead of him, Gwen crept along a narrow ledge he wasn't looking forward to traversing. Gravel crunched beneath her feet. Usually as sure-footed as a mountain goat, she stumbled, swayed and fought to regain her footing.

He lunged forward even as the weight of the pack helped pull her sideways. With a cry, she fell.

RAFE COULDN'T SEE HER. Anguish riding him, he rushed forward faster than he should have and knelt to look over the edge. She sprawled, unmoving, maybe thirty feet down. She hadn't tumbled as far as she could have, but she'd probably bounced off rock outcroppings, and she'd landed on what looked like the remnants of a rock fall. Her head pointed uphill, as if she'd struggled to right herself until the end. He saw no apparent soil, except here and there a few scrubby trees had dug roots deep.

She wasn't dead. She couldn't be.

He looked around frantically, needing to get to her. It was too steep to go directly down unroped, but he saw a zigzag path that might work. It required all his discipline to walk carefully. He wanted to run; he wanted to slide down to reach her side.

Every time he looked, he hoped she'd moved. A groan would have been music to his ears. But there was nothing.

He didn't even want to *think* about how long this was taking. Ten minutes? Fifteen?

What can you do for her when you do get there? an inner voice seemed to mock. *She* was the medic.

Rafe gritted his teeth. When she regained consciousness, she could tell him what to do for her.

He had to be especially careful the last few feet, given the precipice waiting if a hand-or toehold failed. But finally he made it, dropped the tote and squatted next to her.

"Gwen!" he called hoarsely. "Damn it, Gwen, talk to me!"

He rested his fingers on her neck, for a moment not feeling anything. With his own heart beating so damn hard and his hand shaking, would he be able to? Relying on sheer will-power, he calmed himself.

"Gwen." Not so calm. His voice was as grav-elly as the ground beneath her.

But he felt the flutter of her pulse. She was alive. He'd thank God, except she could have broken her neck or back, have suffered a head injury that had her in a coma. He didn't dare remove the pack yet, but he was able to extract the sleeping bag. No matter what, she'd be in shock and unable to hold on to her own body warmth. What's more, the sun's downward path was becoming noticeable.

He tucked the down sleeping bag around her, then stroked hair away from her forehead, his fingertips rough against her smooth skin. He delved into her hair, his touch as delicate as he could manage, searching for any lumps.

Yeah, there was a goose egg not far back from her right temple. Was he seeing swelling and discoloration starting on her temple and reaching down toward her eye, too?

"I need you to talk to me." He swallowed. "Tell me where you're hurt."

Nothing.

What if the helicopter returned now?

They'd be dead, that's what. Even so, he took the handgun from the small of his back and laid it on the ground within reach.

Focus.

He ran his hands down her legs, not finding any obvious breaks. Up her spine and to her neck, which scared him the most. Did she have a cervical collar in the supplies she'd brought? He didn't remember seeing anything like that.

At a soft moan, his gaze snapped to her face. Her lips had parted.

"That's it, sweetheart," he murmured. "I know you must hurt, but you have to talk to me."

She mumbled something.

He bent his head closer. "What?"

"Don't…wanna."

"I know," he said softly. "Do you know where you are? Who I am?"

Her lips unmistakably formed his name.

"That's right. You fell. I…can't tell how badly you're hurt, except that you lost consciousness."

She seemed to be trying to dampen her lips. "Head hurts."

"Yeah. You have a hell of a lump." He slipped his fingers into her hair again and touched it lightly. "You scared me." *You're still scaring me.*

Her lashes fluttered; her face scrunched, and her eyes opened to slits as if she couldn't handle full daylight.

All Rafe could do was stroke her cheek and wait.

"…seen?"

Seen? He abruptly realized what she meant. Yeah, they were exposed to anyone from above on the ridge or, as he feared most, if the helicopter made another pass over. There was nothing to be done about that yet.

"We're exposed," he admitted, "but first things first. Can you tell me where you hurt besides your head?"

Her shoulders moved. She flexed each leg hesitantly, one at a time.

"I'd like to get this pack off you, but I'm not sure you should move yet."

"It…saved me."

The hell it had.

"The weight pulled you off the ledge."

She rolled her head to see him better.

"Don't move!"

"Neck…feels…okay."

He growled a couple of words he should have kept to himself.

"Hit…rocks, but the pack…protected me." Her speech was clearer all the time. "It…snagged. So I didn't fall as far. As fast."

She'd fallen in two segments. That's what she was saying. A strap on the pack catching on a small tree growing out of a crack, or maybe a sharp outthrust rock, really had saved her life.

Rafe sank onto his butt as if the adrenaline that had kept him crouching beside her had been expelled. Until this moment, he hadn't realized the stress his position had put on his wounded thigh.

"Okay." He sounded worse rather than better. "Let me do the work taking it off."

She obeyed, staying mostly still as he gently worked the straps over her shoulders and down her arms. Finally setting the pack aside, he put his hands on her back, moving them up and down, kneading the muscles between her neck and shoulders. "Where does it hurt?"

"Everywhere," she said so quietly he hardly heard her, "but mostly my head. I…think I'm okay. Just…a little battered."

"You were unconscious."

"If I sit up, I can take some Tylenol."

"You need the good stuff more than I do now," Rafe said grimly.

"Not…a good idea after a concussion."

He wanted to argue but had read or heard that before.

"Let me help you."

When she moved, he took most of her weight. Once she lay on her back, they paused, but since she hadn't gasped in pain, he continued to support her as she sat up.

Keeping his arm behind her, he said, "You scared at least ten years off my lifespan."

Was that a faint laugh? "Me too."

They sat quietly for a minute, but the still bright sunlight and sense of exposure made his skin crawl.

He took out a bottle of water and found the Tylenol in her tote bag, shaking out a couple onto his palm and offering them to her.

Gwen swallowed them, sighed and said, "We're mostly at the bottom."

"You took a plummeting elevator."

"Not recommended."

"No." He hesitated. "I hate the idea of making you go on, but we have to get as far as the trees."

"I know. I can do it."

The words were strong, but what he saw on her face scared him in a different way. The swelling and discoloration were worsening, and her eyes, darker than they ought to be, seemed to have sunk deeper yet. Her skin wasn't a healthy shade, despite the tan.

But they couldn't stay here. The risk was too high. He had to push her when he hated the very idea. They had to get under cover. He'd carry her if he had to. He wanted to believe he could despite his injuries and silenced any doubting voice.

He urged a handful of dried fruit on her, since eating seemed to settle people in shock, and finally boosted her to her feet.

Her eyes dilated, then became glassy. He couldn't make her continue hiking. He might kill her. But after standing very still for a minute or two, she blinked hard a few times and straightened.

"I'll carry both bags." He made sure his voice had no give. "I want you to hold on to my arm."

She swallowed and finally dipped her undoubtedly throbbing head a tiny bit. Too soon, they set off, one slow step at a time, as Rafe wished he had an earbud that received intel from a teammate situated to be his extra eyes.

With him and Gwen both severely injured, the danger had just expanded exponentially.

Chapter Eleven

Reasonably alert at first, Gwen understood why Rafe guided her the way he did.

The slope remained quite steep, the footing either irregular over remnants of a volcanic flow or chutes filled with small rocks that slid from beneath the soles of her shoes. When he stopped and turned her almost back the way they'd come, letting her go long enough to move to the downside before gently propelling her forward again, she thought, *Switchback. Smart.*

No more elevator.

Awareness of what he intended along with realizing her body was one solid mass of bruises and strained muscles faded into nothing so concrete. Her head pounded as if a jackhammer was trying to break apart a road surface to clear it away before laying a new one. She wasn't quite sure how she stayed upright, then didn't care if she really was. Rafe's arm wrapped around her, and occasionally he lifted her with the strength of only that arm when he must have doubted whether she could pick up one foot or the other enough to step over an obstacle. Was she leaning on him?

Maybe.

Time blurred. She heard his deep, often gravelly voice but didn't even try to make out words. If she wanted anything in the world, it was to sink to the ground, but the iron bar of his arm kept her upright, and her feet kept moving without any conscious order from her.

They went on, and on. His voice grew more insistent, but she could concentrate on only the one thing. Her next step and the one after that.

When he wrapped her more fully in those strong arms to stop her, she didn't understand. She lifted dazed eyes to him.

"Talk to me."

Was that what he'd been saying all along?

"Sit?" she managed to say.

"We can do better than that. As soon as I get the pad and sleeping bag spread out, you can lie down. Here." Once again, he took command of her body until she found herself sitting on the loamy ground that she began to realize was a forest floor.

Never docile, she didn't know if she could so much as lift a hand. Rafe whipped out the pad and sleeping bag, spreading them right next to her, unlaced Gwen's athletic shoes and eased her over onto the softer layers and onto her back.

She moaned in relief, wriggling her toes, and stared straight upward. The trees rearing above were larger than any they'd yet seen. On many, the lowest branches were far above her head. A squirrel watched her with bright eyes before disappearing in a flash.

Gwen transferred her gaze to the man sitting beside her. *So beautiful*, she thought, despite the lines carved deeper into his cheeks and forehead. The worried way he watched her gave her the strength after all to lift a hand and let it flop onto his hard thigh, the only part of him she could reach.

"All right," she muttered.

"God." He bent his head, but he also seized hold of her hand and held on tight, almost painfully so.

She hoped he never let go.

GWEN DRIFTED OFF to sleep. Rafe didn't move for a long time, watching for every twitch and flicker of an eyelash, at first afraid she wasn't asleep at all, but unconscious. At last, she tried to turn onto her side, convincing him this was a natural sleep. He yanked clothes out of the pack indiscriminately, bundled them up and placed the makeshift pillow under her head.

Then he left her long enough to push his aching body into action to walk a perimeter to be sure no obvious dangers lurked, and that there wasn't anything convenient, like a cave, in case they had to bolt.

No such luck, but at least they couldn't be seen from above, neither from the helicopter nor someone searching with binoculars from the ridge above.

Once he'd returned to their small camp, he started setting up. He didn't want to do this in the fast-approaching darkness. It took him a lot longer than it would have Gwen to get the tent up, simple as it was, but he managed. The stove, he fumbled, but had it ready to heat two more meals from Kimball's stash once Gwen woke up.

His stomach rumbled enough that he did some snacking on nuts and dried fruit, but limited his intake. Who knew how much longer they'd have to stumble around in this primeval wilderness before they were able to contact anyone to call for rescue? They should start portioning out the food more carefully.

As Gwen continued to sleep, he took everything out of the pack and examined it, unfortunately not finding anything he hadn't already seen. He repacked more carefully, with an eye to squeezing in necessities from Gwen's tote bag. They'd have to discard more yet, but he wasn't going to root through her personal possessions without her, much less make that kind of decision.

She didn't stir until the sky had turned a deep purple.

The movement had him turning toward her. She scrunched her face up and mumbled, "Ugh."

Yeah, that about said it all. He couldn't help a silent laugh that cut off quickly as he waited to see how alert she'd be.

"Hey," he said, and she blinked bemusedly his way before starting to push herself up. He reached out to help her.

An owl hooted, and she swiveled her head to look around them. "How long have I been asleep?" She made another of those faces he'd think were cute if it weren't for the distortion caused by swelling. "How would you know?"

"I'm guessing four hours, given how close it is to full darkness. How do you feel?"

How she felt was that she needed privacy. He walked her to her chosen tree, stepped away, then gave her his arm when she reappeared, looking flustered.

After that, he encouraged her to eat a handful of the snack mix and swallow some water before taking more Tylenol.

"I guess if I said I feel fine, you'd know I was lying, huh?" she said unexpectedly.

"Yeah. You lost consciousness long enough to be a real worry."

"The headache is the biggest problem. Otherwise, I think mostly I have bruises."

"Like head to toe?"

"Not quite that bad."

He cocked an eyebrow at her to express his opinion of her upbeat evaluation of her own condition. She quit trying.

They agreed on another of the freeze-dried meals, and he fired up the stove. Since he hadn't seen any running water or heard a stream all afternoon, it was a good thing they'd filled a couple of bottles with water and treated it midday. He decided to dispense with any scrubbing except for his teeth, and would encourage her to do the same. A cup of coffee tonight and another in the morning would do more for both of them than a sponge bath.

Their surroundings dimmed rapidly. She turned on the flashlight a couple of times as he dished up the meal and then made the coffee, but otherwise they sat side by side on the sleeping bag, indulging in long silences but also talking in odd spurts.

Not about today or tomorrow. Gwen didn't bring up the subject of Bill or Bruce Kimball or the map. She told him a few stories from her working life: about delivering a baby in the helicopter, about transporting two men who'd been in a shoot-out and who kept trying to break the restraints to resume their conflict.

"Best friends, one of the wives said. And they were trying to kill each other. What could be worth that?"

Rafe's first thought was that one might have caught his wife in bed with the friend. There'd be two betrayals there, but he personally would consider his wife's the greater.

If he ever married…

After a suitable silence, Gwen asked softly, "Did you grow up with a best friend?"

"Yeah," Rafe said gruffly. The memories and the pain only occasionally jabbed at him. Mostly, they'd dulled.

She didn't ask a question or even turn her head, as if expecting him to elaborate. She'd let it drop if he didn't say anything, Rafe felt sure. She'd been open enough, though, that he felt a twinge of guilt. And really, what difference did it make if he bled a little for her?

"Mateo and I were friends from second grade on, after his mom moved with him and his little sister to live in my school district." Rafe wondered now and again what had become of Ileana but hadn't let himself try to find out. It probably wasn't anything good.

"My parents didn't pay much attention to what I was doing or where I was. Mateo's mom didn't, either, because she worked two jobs. He was supposed to be watching over his sister, but when she got old enough, he decided she could take care of herself."

Gwen was looking at him now. Rafe could feel her regard more than he could make out her features.

"By the time we were fourteen, fifteen, we'd gotten sucked into a gang. At first it was a lot of strutting, wearing the right kind of kick-butt boots and bandannas. Feeling tough. As we got older, closer to graduating, we were expected to do some things." He stared ahead at the trunks of trees he could barely make out. "I started to get cold feet. I think he did, too, but he wanted to belong more than I did. I was afraid I'd be killed if I tried to walk away. He stood with the gang. We had a fight. I'd always believed we'd have each other's backs forever."

Slim, cold fingers slipped into his hand, shaped into a near fist. He squeezed her hand harder than he probably should have.

"When I made noises about walking away, eight or ten of the guys took turns beating me.

I ended up in the hospital, lying to my parents about what had happened. At around the same time, our gang and another had been butting heads. I was still recuperating when a war erupted and Mateo was killed. He was found with drugs on him. I guess he got interrupted before he could deliver them."

"Was he using?" she asked softly.

He cleared his throat. "Yeah. By that time, he was. When I could, I went to see his mom. She knew I'd been part of it, and she screamed at me and then slammed the door in my face. I…waylaid Ileana after school one day, and she gave me a look I'll never forget." To this day, his throat clogged whenever he remembered.

Gwen's head tipped to rest momentarily against his upper arm. The generosity of her touch meant enough to make him uncomfortable. She could get to him. He wasn't sure he wanted that—or dared let himself soften to such an extent.

"My parents were sorry to hear about Mateo. It never occurred to them that I'd been taking the same road. As it was, I headed off to college, got summer jobs or internships that meant I was never home for more than a couple of a weeks at a time, and I dodged any chance of being seen by my former compatriots. Mom and Dad didn't understand my decision to go into law enforcement, and especially when I chose the DEA, but, uh…"

"That's what you intended from the minute you learned about your friend's death."

"Yeah." Hearing how rough his voice had become, he decided he'd said enough. In fact, he released her hand and rose to his feet.

"Time to get some sleep." If he sounded brusque, so be it. "How's your head feel?"

DESPITE THE FACT that she'd had a lengthy nap not that long ago, Gwen felt sure she could sleep again, no problem. She'd taken as much Tylenol as she dared, so there was no point complaining about the drilling still going on in her skull.

She and Rafe briefly discussed whether to set up the tent and agreed they didn't need it. Through the dense lace of the forest canopy, they could make out astonishingly bright stars against a velvety black sky.

Rafe said tersely, "Unless rain is a possibility, I'd prefer to be able to better hear and see what's approaching."

Thank you for the reminder.

Of course, she couldn't disagree. He was already easing into the sleeping bag when she suddenly said, "I didn't have a chance to give you your shot this afternoon. I can—"

"No. I did okay. My injuries aren't the kind

that require continuing on a painkiller as powerful as morphine."

She stood above him, not moving. "I know that, but you weren't in any shape to leap up and go on the run in the mountains, either!"

"I'm not sure I could have that first day," he admitted, his voice a deep rumble that made her think of the purr of a big cat.

Why did he sound gentle? Did he think she needed soothing? If she hadn't proved her competence by now—

"Are you coming?" Nice segue into impatient.

Her response was wordless and grouchy, which she felt a little bad about. Only…she was entitled! Most of her body still hurt. The pad beneath the sleeping bag was maybe half an inch thick. She was grateful for it—really, she was—but she was starting to crave a fat memory foam mattress.

Living long enough for luxuries to be any kind of possibility had to be their priority, she reminded herself. Rafe hadn't whined, and neither would she.

"Yeah," she said, and lowered herself to her hands and knees to begin the backward squirm to fit herself into the limited space left after his big body filled most of it.

The awkwardness seemed to be missing tonight, though. Maybe she just felt too miserable to care about anything like that. And maybe it was the way he helped her, hands careful, until she settled with a sigh, her back to his front so that he spooned her. He held out his arm to provide a perfect resting place for her head, and the heat he seemed to emit all the time was seductive enough that she had to make an effort to hold some small distance between them.

Once she fell asleep…well, she wouldn't know, and neither would he. At least, until morning, when they were bound to be intertwined like ivy climbing a solid brick building.

She took responsibility for pulling up the zipper, necessitating some more wriggling, then relaxed.

"G'night," Rafe murmured, his breath stirring her hair. Unless she was imagining things, he hugged her.

"Good night," she whispered, and closed her eyes, pondering how few times in her life she'd ever slept wrapped in a man's arms, and why this felt so different. So…comforting.

She tried to think about the ultimately tragic story he'd told about his childhood and his best friend, but didn't get any further than picturing a young, possibly lanky Rafe with a bandanna tied around his head, his black hair longer.

Maybe even brushing his shoulders? Tough guy, but not as much as he'd imagined.

What things had he been asked to do? How many had he persuaded himself to do before the values he'd been raised with had kicked in? Did he imagine that if he'd been with Mateo when the gang war broke out, he'd have been able to save his best friend?

Wasn't that what he'd been trying to do ever since?

Feeling fuzzy, Gwen sighed and let herself snuggle just the tiniest bit into the hard curve of Rafe's body. Then she slept.

RAFE HAD TO readjust Gwen a couple of times during the night. The first time, he woke up to discover his dream had prompted the erection he had pressed to her firm but still well-rounded behind. Or maybe it was the other way around. She made some grumbly noises but never really woke up as he eased himself to his back with her partially sprawled over his chest. It took some willpower to persuade his body to subside, given that he still had an armful of sexy, brave, compassionate woman. He must have managed, because he did fall asleep again, this time to a pale dawn and the discovery that Gwen had somehow squirmed her way entirely on top of him.

Her face was pressed into the crook between his neck and shoulder. Her toes flexed against his shins. With him able to feel every curve and dip between, his body had reacted with enthusiasm.

Rafe held himself very still, listening to her slow, even breathing. He didn't feel any need to move even though he'd been fully alert from the moment he opened his eyes. Why not enjoy the pleasure of a harmless arousal?

For all that he relaxed, his mind was always determined to puzzle over every hint of anyone's motivation, including his own. And what he realized was that, beyond the straightforward lust, he felt something more that he hardly recognized: contentment. A quiet sense of peace, as if all were right with his world.

His cynical side kicked in with no trouble. So much had gone wrong in the past three days, he couldn't count all the disasters on one hand. Maybe not even on two. Had she drugged him during the night, and he just hadn't noticed?

Rafe knew better, but he was disconcerted enough by the strange mood that he immediately tensed, shifted Gwen to the side and squirmed out of the sleeping bag.

Peace.

He'd half hoped she would keep sleeping but wasn't surprised after he'd gotten dressed to see that she had sat up and was pushing her tangled hair back from her face. Apparently, the elastic she'd used to keep it tamed in an increasingly disheveled braid had disappeared altogether. It might have looked sexy if not for the bruises on her face.

"It's early," she observed.

"Yeah, sorry to wake you." He'd been about to go use the facilities but paused. "How do you feel?"

Her eyes were clear, no longer dazed, the best sign he could have hoped for.

"Not bad." She grimaced. "My back hurts. And I still have a headache."

"You slept well."

"I guess I must have," she said in bemusement. "Unless I went sleepwalking."

Amused, he said, "Nope. I'd have noticed that."

She gave him a crooked smile that didn't succeed at being as upbeat as she may have meant it to be, given the deep lines between her brows and the furrows on her forehead.

After deciding priority one was bringing her Tylenol and water to wash it down, he did that much before disappearing for a few minutes.

He came back to find she'd washed down the pills but otherwise hadn't moved.

"We should make an early start. Just…give me a few minutes," Gwen said.

Not fooled, he squatted to her level and studied her more carefully. He didn't like this idea but had to offer it.

"We have enough food. What if we rest for the day?"

She fired back, "You mean, what if *I* rest for the day. We didn't sit around when you were in worse shape than I am."

"I didn't have a concussion," Rafe said bluntly. "You slept especially heavy last night. You picked at your food." He'd finished her portion last night. "Be honest. How does a big breakfast sound?"

She scrunched up her face, then winced. "Bacon and eggs?"

"What if I said yes?"

Her chin lifted. She wanted to tell him to bring it on, he could tell, but she finally sighed. "I'm queasy."

"That's what I thought." He frowned at her. "We're tucked away pretty well here."

"I don't remember much after I fell, but that side of the ridge was mostly rock. We had to have been in plain sight for at least a couple of hours, if not more. Especially as slow as I must have been once you picked me up and put me back together."

"That's…a worry," he agreed. He'd been preoccupied by her, too, and not as observant as he usually would be.

Staying put on the assumption they *hadn't* been seen was a gamble, but he also hated to put her at any more risk than she already was.

Chapter Twelve

"We have to keep moving." Gwen dug in stubbornly, but Rafe didn't argue too hard even though he also didn't appear happy. He had to know she was right; they didn't dare laze the day away, giving any pursuers time to catch up.

Or, as he'd pointed out once, even worse would be walking into an ambush because they'd allowed those cold-blooded creeps to get ahead of them.

After insisting he handle packing up, Rafe seemed to dawdle. Gwen defied him by drying the couple of dishes he'd already washed and dismantling the stove. She refused to admit to Rafe how lousy she really felt after the amazing stoicism he'd displayed the first day. She might have worried he could see right through her, except once he'd conceded the argument, he noticeably retreated. For a while, he seemed to pretend she wasn't there at all.

He did finally urge her to help consolidate

what was left in the tote bag with the contents of the pack. "I'd rather you didn't have to carry anything."

In the end, she looked in dismay at her discard pile.

"The rules are that if you carry it in, you carry it out."

"Our situation is extreme."

"Yes, but..." Seeing his impatience, she gave up, but she did insist on burying the bag to the best of their ability, considering their lack of a shovel.

She had a feeling Rafe cooperated only out of a reluctance to leave any trace of their presence behind.

Given that they had no compass, and she had no memory of which way they'd come, she had to depend on his sense of direction. Although, passing through a grove of large trees that they had to wind between made her wonder in a short while whether they might be going in a circle.

Pride kept her walking, with only one break in her composure. She had to lurch behind a tree to empty her stomach of the small amount of breakfast she'd managed to eat. Rafe's expression was so grim when she returned, she avoided meeting his eyes.

"I'm all right."

He didn't say a word.

Since he stepped back to let her go ahead this time, she felt his gaze boring into her back. Excellent incentive for keeping her shoulders squared and her throbbing head high.

They couldn't have been on their way an hour when he said, "Let's take a break."

Gwen didn't argue or even comment. She wondered if the Tylenol she'd taken earlier had been absorbed before she puked, but decided she didn't dare double up. Sitting down on a huge, ancient fallen tree, if only for a few minutes, was a massive relief.

Staring into the shadows of the forest, he said, "I'm depending on you to tell me when you need to stop. Even lie down and close your eyes for a while."

"I'm not sleepy."

"The more rest—"

She huffed out a breath. "I took a four-hour nap yesterday, then we went to bed as soon as the sun went down. I think it's safe to say I've had plenty of sleep!"

He scowled at her, which was the most expression she'd seen on his face since she woke up. She didn't think she'd behaved especially badly this morning. Was this fallout because he'd told her more last night about himself than he'd intended to? Or did *he* hurt more than he wanted to admit? Maybe now that *he* felt stronger, he would become impatient with their slow pace.

Heck, maybe he hadn't gotten any sleep at all, given that he couldn't so much as roll over with her wrapped around him like an invasive vine.

Would he tell her what was going on in his head if she asked?

A little brooding of her own coupled with the brief rest, and she decided there wasn't any reason not to discuss options.

"Maybe we should rethink the plan to stay together. What if *you* go on and leave me hunkered down here instead of the other way around?"

This scowl made him appear forbidding. "Don't be ridiculous! If anyone saw us yesterday, they now know about you. Do you really think I'd leave you?"

"How should I know? You're not being very… communicative."

"Maybe I think it's a good idea for us to try to be quiet."

Because she never shut up? Starting to get mad, Gwen opened her mouth but forgot what she'd intended to say when he abruptly cocked his head and lifted a hand in a stop gesture.

She didn't hear a thing, certainly not an approaching helicopter, but she froze, holding her breath.

With a suddenness she could never have predicted, Rafe tackled her backward over the log. At almost the same instant he fell on top of her, a distinctive *crack* rang in her ears, and bark splintered just above them.

RAFE FOUGHT TO free himself of the pack. Damn this soft ground! He'd never hear footsteps. He didn't even know whether a sound or hint of movement had triggered his alarm in the first place.

Face inches from hers, he murmured, "Once I return fire, throw yourself into those ferns. I think it's a well around the tree that would give you some protection."

Eyes wide and dark, she bobbed her head. He hoped like hell he hadn't hurt her by flattening her, but there'd been no choice.

He pushed himself up enough to half crawl forward, leaving her free to move. Once he'd opened some distance from her, he lifted his Glock and took a few blind shots. A startled sound came to his ears.

Behind him, Gwen squirmed away.

A flurry of shots tore into the rotting log they'd taken cover behind as well as a tree above his head. Bark flew, some peppering his face.

He flicked a glance back. Thank God Gwen had disappeared. He edged forward another few feet.

Would these bastards be wearing bulletproof vests? He'd guess they weren't. The things were hot and uncomfortable, and these kinds of enforcers were more likely to lift weights to achieve impressive muscles than run or hike to stay in shape.

A faint whisper of sound gave him a target even though the bright green camouflage blended too well. He fired even before he'd raised himself high enough to see the SOB not twenty-five feet away. Marking himself as a dead man walking, the bastard's eyes were narrowed on the cluster of ferns surrounding the giant cedar, but he had already started swinging toward Rafe.

Not fast enough. Rafe pulled the trigger with the instinct honed by endless hours at the range. Once, twice, three times.

The man shouted, fired wildly as he staggered and then crashed down with as much force as one of these trees would have if a saw severed it from its roots.

A flicker of movement almost gave Rafe time to dive for cover again, but the second man was already firing. A sting told Rafe he'd at least been grazed by a bullet as he dove sideways.

A series of shots coming from a different direction had him rolling to look behind him. If the four men had joined together—

But what he saw was Gwen, who'd popped into sight like a genie from a bottle and was firing with the same assurance she had when she brought down Kimball.

This second man's face went through the same stages as Kimball's had, too: astonishment, agony…and a vacancy Rafe had seen too many times in his career.

GWEN TRIED TO keep holding the gun steady but saw that her hands shook as if she had a raging fever. Her teeth chattered, too.

Out of the corner of her eye, she saw Rafe rise to his feet as lithely as if he'd never been hurt and rotate in a circle, his own weapon still held in front of him in firing position. He surveyed their surroundings with that hard expression she'd seen so rarely. She suspected that, despite the dim green-tinted light here in the dense forest, he saw more sharply than she ever had, too. Finally, he approached the man he'd shot, kicked his handgun away and stared down at him, then approached the man she'd shot and did the same.

Once she really looked at that body, she couldn't look away. Even from here, she saw the blood and a hole in his temple.

Slowly, her hands dropped. The next thing she knew, she was retching violently, nothing but thin bile coming up, but she couldn't seem to stop.

She'd killed again. How could she have done that?

How could she not?

Rafe prowled out of her sight. He was gone long enough that she assumed he was searching to be sure these two had no nearby backup. When he at last reappeared, he carried a camouflage print pack over one shoulder and a second one with his free hand.

He dropped them both and came to her, dropping to his knees in front of her. She hadn't realized she still held the gun in a tremulous grip until he gently relieved her of it.

"You're not hurt?" he said.

She shook her head, reminding her just how much her head ached. That didn't count.

"I… They followed us."

"Yeah." He cleared his throat. "Lucky we stopped. Otherwise, we'd have had no cover at all."

"No." They might have been gunned down from behind and died. Just like that. Just like… With her gaze compulsively drawn back to the face of the man she'd killed, she had dry heaves.

Rafe rubbed her back. When she raised her

head, he smoothed her hair back from her forehead with a completely steady hand, in con-
trast to hers. *He often did that*, she thought,
and imagined how wild and tangled her hair
must be by now.

"C'mon." He reached out a hand. "Let me
pull you up."

As he had guessed, the ferns had disguised
a hole around the tree trunk. She'd essentially
fallen into it and had fought to right herself fast
enough to be able to provide backup. As shaky
as she felt, she was grateful for the strength that
swung her up as if she weighed nothing.

She probably *had* lost weight, she thought,
her mind inexplicably drifting. *What a diet
plan*, she thought.

Rafe settled her on the log again so that her
back was to the dead men.

"Let's go through their packs quickly and
see whether there's anything that will help us.
Otherwise, later we can try to pinpoint where
we left them."

"Their guns?"

"We'll take those."

Because he thought they might still need
them? Or because he didn't want a backcountry hiker stumbling on them?

Did his motives matter?

She wasn't an awful lot of help, mostly watching as he transferred first a pair of wallets and then some food to their own pack.

"We could take a second sleeping bag," he offered, sounding oddly neutral, "although that would probably mean carrying a second pack, too."

"If you'd prefer that…"

"No. I thought you might."

She couldn't imagine nights not having the comfort of his arms around her. "No," she whispered.

His eyes caught hers for an unnerving moment. The creases in his forehead betrayed a perturbation she couldn't read. Did he think she might be cracking up?

Was she?

No.

She quit bothering to watch him sort. When he said, "Let's cover some distance before we stop for a bite to eat," she stood up before Rafe could help her. The idea of eating didn't entice her, but she'd have to try at some point, wouldn't she?

THOUGH THE PACK was now weighed down by four handguns—two full-size, two smaller backup weapons—as well as a few supplements to his wardrobe and to their diet, Rafe was barely conscious of it. He focused primarily on Gwen. Even as her drawn face and careful steps that were clumsy compared to her usual grace scared the hell out of him, he felt unfamiliar pride in her strength and the intense concentration that kept her moving forward despite what had to be a world of pain. Out of necessity he also listened for any sound coming from behind that wasn't natural. And, of course, for the hum of helicopter rotors.

He brooded about why he hadn't found a SAT radio. Why wouldn't they have carried one to stay in touch with the other pair and their base? Once the men on the ground spotted him and Gwen, you'd think they'd have called in backup. He'd located one cell phone, but it had been locked by fingerprint or some other method that made it as useless as Gwen's phone with the drained battery. Had it worked to reach whatever airbase the helicopter was flying out of?

It was also possible, he reflected, that none of these men was aware that cell phones didn't work in much of the park. Unless they'd hiked or climbed here, why would they? To most Americans, the idea that there were still wild parts of their own country where their precious mobile phones became useless baggage was unthinkable.

He'd noted on the map he and Gwen carried that they might be coming in reach of cell phone towers to the north, although plenty of mountainous terrain could still be interfering. Unless the helicopter showed up again in the near future, Rafe's intent was to get Gwen and himself to a trail where they might find hikers with working cell phones.

Between trees, he saw water glinting blue ahead. The lake nestled in a bowl in the land, but he suspected it was still at a significant elevation. The water was startlingly clear, the shores rocky.

Some serious work remained ahead of them to climb more ridges or to see if it was possible to follow one of the streams he remembered noting on the map that meandered to ultimately join the west fork of the White River. What Gwen had called the Northern Loop Trail crossed the west fork at one point.

Otherwise, the distance wasn't great to another pair of lakes to the south with a backcountry campground and even a park ranger patrol cabin marked on the map, but the scrambles over more ridges might be beyond Gwen's capability now. What Rafe knew was that they wouldn't make it today. This was as good a place to stop as any, although they needed to retreat back into the trees so as not to be seen from above.

Predictably, she said, "I can go on," but Rafe shook his head.

"One more day, we should make it to that patrol cabin. We don't have enough hours of daylight left today."

"I don't think there's always a ranger at those cabins."

His mouth tightened. "There's also a camp-ground marked."

"The kind with something like three or four sites."

"I get that. But from that point, our odds improve of meeting someone with a working phone, or a charger you can use."

"Yes. You're right." She looked around with unsettling vagueness. "Here?"

"Looks good enough to me."

He wished he had any idea *which* lake they'd found, but it was pretty. One shore was wooded enough, somebody would have to stumble over them to find them—unless, like the dead men, they'd been tracking him and Gwen.

He shied away from thinking about the two corpses they'd left to the mercy of the wildlife. The glassy look in Gwen's eyes either meant she, too, was picturing them or that her concussion was deeper than he'd believed.

As soon as he lowered the pack to the ground, he extracted the sleeping bag and pad and spread them out. A glance at the sky found a scattering of clouds, but whether they suggested rain tonight, he couldn't tell. For now, he just wanted Gwen to lie down.

Once again, he helped lower her to a sitting position. She watched as he knelt, untied her shoes and tugged them off.

Her smile was unexpected. "I can't remember any man who wasn't a shoe salesman taking my shoes off."

He grinned. "If I put them back on in the morning, just to be sure they fit, you know…"

Gwen wrinkled her nose. "Cinderella, I am not."

Rafe wasn't so sure. She was beautiful enough to play the part, although he felt damn sure she wouldn't have ducked her head and obeyed the cruel stepmother no matter what she dished out. Under these circumstances, they'd gotten to know each other in a way a couple might not in a normal relationship, even over the course of months.

He frowned. *This isn't a romantic relationship.* He hadn't had one of those in years. Sex, yes. Letting himself feel hope for the future? No. And he didn't even know why he was thinking about this.

He let that slide, though he wasn't a man who usually let a lie to himself pass.

GWEN WOULD HAVE liked to find a comfortable slab of rock overhanging the lake and lie there watching for minnows. She didn't even try, for too many reasons, starting with the lack of a conveniently placed slab. Placing herself out in the open would have been foolish beyond belief, too. What she *really* wanted, she realized, was for them to be on a backpacking trip for fun instead of being the prey still hunted by a ruthless offshoot of a drug cartel.

She wanted to have saved a life instead of taking two.

Except…she had. Rafe's.

She caught him watching her, as she so often did, and wished his expression wasn't so often unreadable.

He swore suddenly.

Oh, no. She heard it, too—distant but undoubtedly approaching.

"They can't see us even if they fly right overhead!" she cried.

"If they get close, it's because they have a damn good idea where we are," said Rafe, rough voice shaped by familiar grimness.

"You think the four men on the ground stayed in communication? Which means the two we haven't met might know where we are?"

"I do."

Head cocked as she listened, Gwen said, "It's coming fast."

"I want to see it. Where did we stash the binoculars?" He flung a few things out of the pack before locating them.

"I should come, too."

Rafe barely hesitated before nodding. "Bring your gun."

A couple of minutes later, they found a thicket of what Gwen said were huckleberries growing from a rotting stump that showed signs of having burned from a lightning strike or forest fire at some point in the past. Right at the edge of the tree line, they were able to see a stretch of sky above the lake. He'd set his handgun within easy reach, and now lifted the binoculars to his eyes.

The helicopter snapped into sharp focus minutes later as it buzzed a lower elevation than it did yesterday. It had to be skimming barely over the treetops. A small herd of what Rafe recognized as elk burst from cover onto the lakeshore and ran in great bounds before disappearing again. The damn thing was flying straight enough toward them that his gut tightened.

Through the binoculars, he could just see a couple of men crouched in the open side door, rifles raised. Fury struck Rafe. Enough was enough. He was going to bring the whole organization down, if it was the last thing he ever did.

"Do you hear that?" Gwen murmured as if she were afraid they could be overheard.

"What the hell?"

A second later, a much larger helicopter appeared on a trajectory meant to cut off the first one. This second one was painted an army green and displayed what Rafe thought had to be government insignia. Was that a Chinook? Not impossible, considering how near the joint army/air force base of Lewis-McChord was.

The helicopter that was their nemesis abruptly lifted, gained altitude and circled back the way it had come, topping the ridge moments later to take it out of sight. The army helicopter changed path, too, swinging in a wide semicircle in apparent pursuit. Or just aiming to drive an unauthorized intruder past the national park boundaries?

In anguish, Gwen exclaimed, "If only we had a flare!"

"Took the words right out of my mouth," he growled.

Chapter Thirteen

After watching the army helicopter disappear over the treetops and ridge, Gwen had clung very briefly to the hope that it might reappear, might even have been assigned to search for her and Rafe.

Or at least for Rafe.

When twenty or thirty minutes passed and it hadn't returned, she gave up on what had been an unrealistic hope. How would the army have gotten involved?

Upon their return to their camp, Rafe asked that question.

Gwen shrugged. "I've read that they do call in the Chinook helicopters for rescues near the summit where the smaller ones can't go. If it had transferred an injured climber to an ambulance at Paradise or Sunrise or gone all the way to a hospital, there's no reason it would have been out this way, though. It might have been on some kind of training flight and didn't like the looks of an unmarked helicopter flying without clearance in the national park. Or..." Okay, she still had a grain of optimism. "Is there any chance the DEA could have reached out for help searching for the missing helicopter and you?"

Seated now on the sleeping bag beside her, he grimaced. "I doubt it, but...maybe. A search was surely mounted, but probably focused on the planned route."

"That's true, except...you'd think *some*body, somewhere would have seen that plume of smoke."

"If the crash site was located, I think we have to assume Kimball's body had already been removed. If that's so, I'm not sure what regular search and rescue personnel would have made of the burned helicopter. They'd have found the pilot and presumably contacted EMS Flight. They must have known you were on board. Are we sure they knew *I* was?"

She frowned at that. As sketchy as the whole thing was, she couldn't guarantee EMS did. Bill had claimed to be talking to dispatch, so she hadn't answered her phone. What if he'd lied?

And would the hospital who'd sent Rafe as a patient over for transport to Seattle have reason to connect him with a missing helicopter? Would the EMTs who'd loaded him have ever

given that part of their job another thought?
They'd certainly have had no way to suspect
they were part of something secretive.

She told him what she'd been thinking.

"I've had most of the same thoughts, except I
didn't realize your base didn't specifically send
you to take care of me." He shrugged. "We'll
know more once I can talk to Zabrowsky."
Rafe's mouth quirked. "If he's able to snap his
fingers and demand the army pick me up, I'll
be impressed."

Gwen smiled. The never-ending headache
and debilitating exhaustion had temporarily
stolen her ability to laugh. Given a few hours of
rest, she felt sure she'd regain her determination
and maybe even optimism. Look how far they'd
come! Relatively speaking, they didn't have all
that far to go. And, would anyone dare send that
helicopter out again after they'd received what
at least constituted a warning? They'd have to
be desperate.

Which, unfortunately, they seemed to be.

After some discussion about the increasingly
gray sky, Rafe set up the tent and covered it
with the tarp. He cooked dinner, too, which
Gwen hadn't been sure she'd be able to eat. Her
appetite was returning, though, which was good
news. Maybe by morning, the headache would

be gone, too. She made a face. Sad to say, she wasn't *that* optimistic.

When the evening became chilly as the gray of the sky deepened, Rafe urged a parka on Gwen that he'd appropriated from one of the dead men. She wasn't quite squeamish enough to refuse the cozy warmth. He seemed comfortable with a fleece quarter-zip, but it was heavier than hers. Plus, Rafe's natural thermostat had a higher setting than hers did.

They sipped coffee, letting the quiet sink in. An owl's soft hoot was followed by small shrieks as a nocturnal hunter—possibly the same owl—found prey. Rafe made her feel surprisingly safe by his mere presence, and that disturbed her. This was surely one of their last nights together. She had let herself become more...attached than she should. Than was safe, Gwen thought, deliberately echoing the word she'd used a minute ago in her head.

She'd never been a fan of sticking her head in the sand. Better to look straight on at reality. So she asked, in an I'm-just-wondering voice, "What will happen to you once this is over?"

This silence felt quite different. Rafe went still, with the coffee cup halfway to his mouth. Finally, he said, "Unfortunately, I suspect I'll be stashed again in some kind of safe house. I think I told you the trial will likely be at least a year away. Hell, maybe longer than that. After all this, the agency will want to up the protection."

"A dank fortress?"

He smiled faintly.

She asked, "How can you trust the same kind of arrangement after you were betrayed?"

"Not sure I do." He resumed movement, swallowing what appeared to be the rest of the coffee in his cup and then setting it down before he turned his head to look at her. He didn't have a lot of the tells most people did, the kind that would give away his real thoughts, and the oncoming darkness didn't help.

"So?" she asked softly. Whispered, really.

He shook his head. "I may have no choice. Even if I could get away with it, I can't walk away. I want to bring these scumbags down like you wouldn't believe. For the victims of the drug trade in general, for the guys who were gunned down guarding me, for that pilot who didn't know what he was getting into and now for *you*."

Her heart did something odd that made her briefly light-headed. No, she couldn't let herself believe for a minute that he was suggesting…what it sounded as if he was suggesting.

"You've saved me as often as I've saved you" was the best retort she could offer.

To her shock, he took her hand even as he said huskily, "This isn't all about our body count, or who has picked up whom the most times."

"You're stuck on the fact that you think I didn't deserve to get sucked into this."

"Partly," he agreed in the deep voice that gave her goose bumps. "Some of it is just because of who you are."

Gwen wanted desperately to ask what he meant by that. He seemed to be inviting the question, which scared her. They would part ways tomorrow or the next day. Soon. Assuming they *were* able to make a phone call to the DEA. Despite what a short time they'd had together, she could care too much about Rafe Salazar. Maybe she already did, but she had to nip it in the bud, or she'd suffer for letting herself fall for him.

"That's nice of you to say," she told him blithely. She was proud of herself for being able to sound so casual.

It worked, too, because after a moment, he released her hand and withdrew into himself.

Her newly chilled fingers curled into a painful fist at her side.

DAMN. IF HE wasn't in love with this woman, he was coming close. No, that was ridiculous. He'd never even kissed her. This was just the kind of intense bond that came into being when you shared a level of danger with someone else. He'd felt it working lengthy operations with fellow agents when they'd all developed complete trust. A few times, one of those agents had been female, so he couldn't blame these disturbing emotions entirely on the fact that Gwen was a woman.

Don't make this into something it isn't, he told himself, but he couldn't push back the crushing sense of dread he felt when thinking about saying goodbye to her.

Either she didn't share these emotions, or she was smart enough to know they couldn't go anywhere. He had to accept that.

It might have been easier if, half an hour later, they didn't have to squeeze into the same sleeping bag and almost effortlessly twine their bodies together as if they'd done this every night for weeks or months rather than mere days.

She didn't say a word after a mumbled "Good night." He didn't know if she felt the kiss he pressed to her head. What he did know was that she didn't surrender to sleep anywhere near as soon as her physical condition suggested she should have. Rafe loved the soft feel of her breasts pressed against his side and chest, her arm crooked over his belly and her hand splayed over his heart. Once she really conked out, she'd lift her leg and lay it across his, too. That she hadn't was one way he knew she was probably brooding the same way he was.

He sure as hell couldn't sleep until he felt her utter relaxation.

It came, eventually, after a soft sigh. He turned his head enough to kiss her forehead, having the wry thought that they'd both have slept sooner if they'd let themselves make love first.

Have sex. Love…was off the table.

The words, *for now*, drifted through his head just before he let himself relax into sleep, too.

As always, his sleep was restless. He'd tuned his radar to pick up any untoward sounds, and given how little time he had spent in the mountains in this part of the world, too many of those sounds triggered brief waking moments. Gwen squirming had the same effect on him, as did what he suspected were a couple of nightmares. Both times, she let out a gasp and stiffened. The second time, she cried out. Whether she actually heard his comforting words or felt him kneading whatever tight muscles he could reach, Rafe didn't know, but she gave no sign of waking up and relaxed back to sleep.

Would she keep having nightmares? Yeah, he'd bet on it. These days of sustained tension and fear provided plenty of material. They might have reawakened nightmares from after the car accident and her mother's death, too.

He had his own share of them. He'd come to think of them as a slideshow. A different one would haunt him every night. They tended to circle around until they replayed. Again and again.

Grimacing at the darkness, he knew damn well he'd added a couple new ones. Being tied securely to a backboard, unable to so much as lift an arm when that greedy sellout, Bruce Kimball, held a gun on him and then, worse, turned it on Gwen—that rose to the top. Watching her fall, unable to reach her... That had been bad, too.

The soft patter of rainfall on the tarp awakened him once, not heavy enough to be a real concern, although if it kept raining tomorrow—today?—the going would be miserable for two people not equipped with rain gear.

He did manage to drop off again, although by morning, he'd swear he'd been lucky to catch half an hour of shut-eye at a time throughout the entire night.

With the pearly light of dawn, he eased himself out of the sleeping bag without quite waking Gwen, who merely grumbled and clutched at him as if someone were stealing her favorite teddy bear.

He hastily dressed even as he looked around. The foliage was damp but no longer dripping, and what he could see of the sky made him think the clouds had cleared. Rafe grunted at the thought that they were lucky. He couldn't label much that had happened recently as lucky.

Except, of course, Gwen.

Growling under his breath, he opened some distance from their campsite to relieve himself, then returned to set up the stove again and put on water to heat for oatmeal and coffee.

RAFE'S MOOD DIDN'T appear to have improved today, although Gwen could hardly blame him. She wondered whether he could possibly have recovered from his gunshot wounds as miraculously as it appeared—or as he made an enormous effort to make it appear.

His face was drawn, hollows noticeable beneath sharp cheekbones. He kept scratching irritably at dark stubble on his jaw and neck that could now be called a beard. She made an effort to brush out the tangles in her hair—along with twigs, leaves and one small slug that she tossed away with a shudder—but the best she could do was pull it back out of her face and hope it didn't look as greasy and sweat-soaked as it had to be.

"What I'd give for a shower," she muttered,

not intending to be heard, but Rafe, who was strapping the tent and sleeping bag to the back-pack, raised his eyebrows at her.

"I'd put living another day ahead of the shower, but both sound good."

She laughed, which made her realize she felt better today. *Better* being a relative term. His mouth quirked briefly in response.

Astonishingly enough, their route today headed downhill. Probably too steeply, so she'd run her fingertip along what looked to be their best path, although really, who knew? Even a topographical map only told you so much.

The zigzag lines of the Northern Loop Trail about where they hoped to join it made Rafe frown.

She said, "That's nothing compared to what we've already accomplished."

He bent to study the map again before saying, "You're right. This'll be a breeze."

She almost smiled again at the wryness in his tone.

Downhill was harder than uphill for aching thigh muscles and creaking joints. Grateful that the rainfall hadn't extended into the morning, Gwen pushed herself as hard as she could and felt guilty that Rafe still carried the pack.

Within an hour, her headache worsened and throbbed in time with every step. Scrambling along the side of a drop-off too steep to permit them to directly descend unroped kept her from being able to sink into the kind of lethargy she had yesterday.

Was it only yesterday that she'd fallen over the cliff? Her memory felt fuzzy enough, she wasn't sure.

Rafe issued curt orders to stop for a break every so often, usually when he spotted a fallen log or rock that allowed them to sit for a few minutes.

Halfway through the day, he suggested they get out the stove and heat water for one of the freeze-dried meals, of which they had plenty, and she could only say dully, "If you want to." None of the nuts or trail mix they had left appealed very much to her.

While he set up and prepared their meals, she refilled their water bottles at the creek they'd reached but hadn't yet figured out how to cross. She dropped purifying tablets in the bottles after returning. When she sat down and accepted a dish, she ate because he insisted on it.

She began to fear that when they actually came to the trail, she'd think it was a mirage.

Both ended up wet, and not just their boots and lower legs, when they scrambled over the rocky bed of the stream tumbling down the steep slope. From the map, she knew they'd had no choice but to cross it somewhere. At least here, it didn't quite qualify as a waterfall.

Midafternoon, when Gwen saw a lake a few hundred feet below them, she wanted to cry. That almost had to be Lake Ethel, didn't it? Which meant…

They'd made it.

Almost made it.

What if they reached the campsite and patrol cabin, and no one was there? She had no idea how long ago the map had been published. Maybe the patrol cabin had been abandoned, burned down—who knew?

What if…?

They'd keep walking, that's what. Once they reached the trail, it should be maintained and therefore mostly smooth, nothing like the country they'd traversed to this point.

Easy peasy, Mom would have said, because *her* mother had said it, too. Except, of course, for having to watch out for the ruthless men still hunting them.

The remaining descent to the lake and the short hike to the neighbouring Lake James, where the campsite was, wasn't as easy as she'd have liked it to be, but Rafe stopped her with a hand on her shoulder.

"I see a couple of backpackers."

"What?" Gwen whirled and made her-

self dizzy. She'd have gone down if he hadn't grabbed for her.

"Okay?"

"I…" She blinked a few times. "Just… shouldn't move so quickly."

He handed her the binoculars she hadn't seen him remove from the pack.

She didn't have to adjust them very much to spot the two hefty brightly covered packs carried by unidentifiable hikers. Unidentifiable, because the tops of their heads could barely be seen over the packs, and they were walking away—northeast, to be exact—taking the switchback descent depicted on the map.

Gwen couldn't see running after them, crying, "Stop! Do you have a phone?"

"Where they are," Rafe observed, "there'll be others."

"Like seeing a mosquito?" she asked politely.

He flashed a grin that weakened her already shaky knees. "Right. Except I'd have said an elk. People are herd animals."

That smile almost erased the lines of tiredness and pain she'd become accustomed to seeing on his lean face. She had to look away. Sky? Blue. One long white tail of vapor left by a jet probably rising from the Seattle airport. No helicopters.

"Let's go." Rafe urged her forward, and she complied.

Just finding the trail was astonishing. They turned right: southwest. She'd been right. The way was not level, but relatively speaking, this was like strolling on a sidewalk. She'd never again think of hiking on designated trails as roughing it.

The campsite was empty.

After a detour to the patrol cabin, ditto. They knocked on the door, opened it and peered in. It looked abandoned.

Rafe muttered something she suspected was stronger than the *damn, damn, damn* Gwen was thinking.

He rolled his head, making her realize that his shoulders, at least, must ache. "Wait here? Or go looking for other backpackers?"

"Go looking. At this time of year, there are bound to be other hikers on a trail talked up in every guidebook."

"You want a bite to eat first?"

"Uh-uh. I'm afraid if I sit down, I won't be able to get myself up again."

Honesty was not, in this case, the best policy. Worry carved grooves in his forehead. "That means you definitely *should* take a break or even stop for the night."

"We can do better than that if only we find

someone with a working phone," she reminded him. "Shower. Bed."

"Helicopter ride."

She had to think about that. Would she start feeling nervous on the job every time the copter lifted off the pad? Surviving a second crash would be pushing her luck. But Gwen had been flying for her job too long. She had...faith. The EMS Bell helicopter wouldn't have gone down as it did if Bill had been left in control.

"A dream come true," she told Rafe, who half smiled, half grimaced and waved a hand ahead.

"You first, Ms. I-Puked-in-Secret-Last-Night."

And she'd thought he hadn't noticed.

Chapter Fourteen

The first backpacker, a lone young guy, looked alarmed at the sight of them. Rafe didn't think they could possibly look *that* bad. He asked, "Do you have a phone?"

The guy shook his head hard and scuttled by them, walking sideways like a crab. "No phone, sorry. There's, ah, some other people back there." He gestured vaguely, then hurried away.

Rafe watched him break into a trot.

Gwen smiled weakly. "Apparently, we could be cast in a horror movie."

"Maybe we're zombies and don't know it."

He was awed that Gwen had found humor in having their hopes dashed. That flash of laughter was gone, though, and now she stood still with her eyes closed, doing nothing but waiting.

He really wanted to get her to a hospital.

Rafe took her hand and squeezed it. "Onward."

Her lashes fluttered and she met his eyes. "Sure."

He wished the trail was wide enough for them to walk abreast, but instead he nudged her ahead. Without a word or a complaint, she went.

He didn't love to discover they were once again climbing, but Gwen trudged on, Rafe sticking close behind in case she hit the wall.

It didn't happen. She was still on her feet, putting one in front of the other, when he heard voices. She did, too, her head coming up.

This time, they were met by a group of four, three men and a woman.

Instead of panic, he saw concern on the face of the guy in the lead.

"What happened to you two?"

Rafe moved up beside Gwen and wrapped an arm around her. She leaned into him slightly.

"We were on a helicopter that crashed in rough country a few days ago. The pilot was killed. We're the only survivors."

All four people stared at them in a kind of awe. "I read something about a medical helicopter disappearing," another of the men said.

"That was us," Rafe agreed. "Is there any chance you have a phone with enough bars to allow us to make a call?"

He, for one, held his breath waiting for the answer.

THE RINGS WERE one of the best things Rafe had ever heard. The snarled "Zabrowsky" might be number two.

"It's Rafe Salazar." He watched as the woman and one of the men convinced Gwen to sit down on a folding camp stool—who knew there was such a thing?—and sip water. The woman had produced a Butterfinger bar that she handed over.

"Salazar?" Rafe's boss sounded genuinely stunned. "Goddamn. I was afraid you were dead. You just…disappeared. If personnel at the hospital were right, you were on that damn helicopter that went down, except there was no trace of you when we did locate it."

Rafe turned his back on the group and lowered his voice. "I was still coming out of anesthesia—couldn't have been long after they let you in to see me—when I found myself being transported to an airfield and loaded onto a rescue helicopter. Supposedly, I was being taken to Seattle for better care at a major hospital. Really, Bruce Kimball had paid off the EMS pilot to rendezvous with someone else in Mount Rainier National Park."

"Kimball?"

"You know him?"

"Vaguely. Was he the one…?"

"Who shot up the safe house? I assume so.

I didn't get a good look, but I know Eaton let the shooter in because he recognized him. Uh, I don't suppose he or Stanton survived?"

The clipped no didn't surprise him.

"I'm on a borrowed phone. The paramedic who saved my life is with me. I'm still hurting, but she's in worse shape now. We'd love a pickup."

Rafe turned, consulted with everyone else and finally conceded that they would be best to go back to the campsite and cabin, where a helicopter could land.

Zabrowsky apparently pulled up a map on his computer and agreed he'd get a bird in the air as quickly as possible.

"Sit tight," he said, and Rafe gave a rough laugh. That sounded a lot better than any of the alternatives.

He handed the phone to the backpacker and said, "Thank you. Our ride will be along. I can't tell you how glad we were to see you."

Their new friends escorted them back to the campsite and insisted on waiting with them. He hesitated briefly, but most often there was safety of a sort in numbers, and even if that damn unmarked helicopter swept overhead, if Rafe and Gwen ducked their heads, they might appear to be part of the group.

All kinds of goodies appeared from the packs,

and he dug out the remaining freeze-dried meals. A hot late lunch and early dinner helped fill the time until Rafe heard the distant, ominous roar of an approaching helicopter—except this one came from the north.

Gwen had a shimmer of tears in her eyes, although she never let them fall. The relief was so profound that Rafe might have shed some tears himself if they'd been alone.

But under it all, a heavy weight had settled in his chest, somewhere under his breastbone. He didn't want to leave Gwen. Say a quick goodbye to her in a hospital ER, say, leaving her to be evaluated while he walked away.

But would he be given a choice?

IT TURNED OUT worse than Gwen had expected. Within seconds of the helicopter landing on the roof of the hospital, medical personnel ran to it. Her protests were ignored when someone wrapped a collar around her neck, she was eased onto a backboard and lifted onto a wheeled gurney. Talking to an older man who had walked out with the hospital employees, a man she presumed to be his boss, Rafe had his back to her when the team around her pushed her at the speed of a trot toward the entrance to the hospital.

Gwen opened her mouth to call to him…

but then closed it. Anguish squeezed her chest. She didn't want more thanks, and would a last, terrible look into his dark eyes really be better than this, a clean severing of their relationship?

No. He was probably glad to hand her off safely. She needed to be glad *he* had made it this far safely, too.

Given what a short time she'd known him, how could parting hurt this much?

All she could do was close her eyes and experience being the patient for the second time in her life. Like most medical professionals, she was terrible at it.

"I'm sure I did have a concussion," she repeated countless times. "But I'm feeling better. I'm not dizzy anymore." Which wasn't quite true, but she just wanted to go home. She identified how many fingers were being held up, stared into the blinding light shone into her eyes and endured the claustrophobia induced by an MRI.

Her doctor, an eager young resident who she recognized from EMS deliveries to this hospital, finally conceded.

"I'm tempted to insist you stay the night, but as long as you go straight home—and not on a bus—" He broke off again to level a stern look at her. "I trust there are no tall flights of stairs in your building."

She almost laughed. She and Rafe had scrambled up thousands of feet in elevation, then down and up again, and now a staircase was supposed to daunt her?

"Elevator," she said.

The doctor frowned at her. "All right. You need to see your own doctor soon. Immediately if your headache worsens, you become dizzy, pass out or you experience difficulty with your vision."

Gwen tuned him out while making sure her expression was pleasant and accepting.

Only as she sat in a wheelchair and allowed an orderly to push her toward the main entrance was she hit by the realization that she couldn't even call for an Uber or pay for a taxi or let herself into her apartment. There had to be a way to reclaim her possessions, specifically, her keys, wallet and phone.

"Wait!" she said.

Almost simultaneously, she heard her name being called from behind her.

"Ms. Allen? Glad I caught you."

It was the man she'd seen on the helipad with Rafe. Iron-gray hair cut short, and the furrows in his face had her placing him in his fifties.

"I'll take over," he announced, firmly edging the orderly aside. "I need to speak to Ms. Allen."

His force of personality won the brief tussle, and she found herself being wheeled back to the elevator.

Once the doors had closed behind them and the elevator was dropping to what had to be a basement level, he introduced himself as supervisory agent Ron Zabrowsky and said, "I'd appreciate it if we could talk for a minute. I know an interview is probably the last thing you want right now—"

"No, it's okay. Is… Has Rafe—Agent Salazar—been checked out by a doctor?"

"Yes, immediately. He's recovered extraordinarily well given his activities this past week. From what he's said, he wouldn't have gotten far without you."

"Strapped to the backboard, he couldn't fight back," she said.

"No."

Was she in trouble for having shot and killed a federal agent?

They exited the elevator at a level that appeared to be deserted. Gwen felt uneasy for the first time. What would this man do if she insisted on walking? Having him behind her, pushing her to an unknown destination, made the hair on the back of her neck prickle. What if *he* had been allied with Bruce Kimball? When she asked Rafe what he thought about his boss, he'd hesitated.

"Where are we going?" she asked.

"Right here." He stepped to the side to open a door, held it with his hip and pushed her inside.

The first thing she saw was the pack lying on a table, a pile of things that had been in it to one side. A doctor rose from a padded office chair, scaring Gwen even more for a fleeting moment.

Then she realized he was *not* a doctor. It was Rafe—tall, sexy and somehow intimidating in undoubtedly borrowed clean blue scrubs to replace his filthy, torn clothing. Why intimidating? She didn't know. It wasn't as if she ever backed down just because a man or woman had the letters MD on an identity badge. She continued to take in Rafe's appearance, from his gleaming hair to the tuft of equally black hair that showed in the V of the scrub top, which bared his powerful arms. Her gaze swept all the way to the familiar borrowed boots.

She blinked back tears. Had *he* insisted on having a chance to say goodbye?

Humor seemed like a better idea than diving into his arms and sobbing.

"You look better than I do."

A grin flickered as he came straight to her. "For some reason, they insisted on cleaning me up before they replaced my dressings." Then his jaw tightened. "I can't believe they're booting you out! You can't tell me you don't have a concussion!"

"No, I did have one, but I don't have any symptoms alarming enough for the doctor to keep me overnight. I was going to take a taxi home, except I suddenly remembered I can't because you have my stuff."

He grinned. "I was holding it hostage so you couldn't get away."

"Oh." She cast a glance over her shoulder to see that Rafe's boss had strolled to a conference table and settled himself close enough to watch them but gave them a measure of privacy.

She lowered her voice. "Do you know yet where you'll be sent?"

Zabrowsky cleared his throat, and she realized that privacy was illusory.

Rafe grimaced. "That's…not yet settled."

She turned a blistering stare on his boss. "It had better be more secure than the last safe house!"

Rafe's crooked smile calmed her. "I'm not liking the idea of any agency safe house right now."

Gwen sniffed. "I can see why, at least until you can be sure Kimball was the only DEA agent willing to sell out."

Both men winced.

"So?" If she sounded acid, she couldn't help

it. "Will you be put up in a hotel under a false identity until somebody comes up with a better solution?"

"You know I can't tell you," he said with the gentle timbre to his voice that always undid her.

Gwen tried to smile. "I know." He'd tried all along to hide how much pain he was in. Feeling vulnerable in any way might have been a new experience for him. Would he hate knowing she still felt protective of him?

She took a deep breath. Of course her idea would be shot down right away, but she decided to throw it out there, anyway. "You'd be welcome to come home with me while the investigation is underway. Who would expect that? Even though I was seen with you, does anyone know who I am?"

Rafe froze. She glanced uneasily at Zabrowsky to see a strange expression on his face.

"My apartment isn't super secure," she said tentatively, "but it's not bad. In theory, no one can get in or use the elevator without an electronic fob. If you stay out of sight..."

"I could be endangering you."

"We've kind of got a mutual aid society going already, don't we? I wouldn't mind having someone do the cooking until I'm feeling a little better."

"You won't be able to go back to work for a while," he said slowly.

Gwen sighed. "No. Even aside from the head injury, I'll be grounded until my ribs fully heal. I will need to let my superior know why I didn't show up to work Monday."

Zabrowsky joined them, half sitting on the conference table. "Surely he or she knows you were on the helicopter that disappeared."

"I'm actually not sure. Dispatch in Yakima offered me a ride along with the pilot to deliver an empty helicopter to Seattle. It's possible even that was kind of under the table. You know, a favor for a coworker. How much anyone higher up the chain knows about the unauthorized patient or Kimball as passenger—and whether I was on the helicopter or not—I won't know until I talk to them. And… I suppose you may want me to limit what I say?"

"We'll talk about that," Zabrowsky agreed.

She frowned. "You did look at the crash site."

"Eventually," he agreed. "I was still in Yakima when I heard some buzz about the medical helicopter that had gone missing, and then several days later, the fact that it had been found way off course, having gone down in the national park. Since supposedly there hadn't been passengers because it was merely being transferred between bases, I couldn't be positive it was connected to Rafe's disappearance. We'd already turned that town upside down and given it a hard shake."

She would bet he was popular with the Yakima PD.

"At the hospital, several people claimed a DEA agent, who'd showed his credentials, had cleared Rafe's transfer to the EMS base and thus to Seattle. Needless to say, the badge did not belong to Bruce Kimball. Somehow, he'd gotten his hands on a badge belonging to an agent who had just retired. So recently—" he grimaced "—it might have been verified if anyone had thought to call to make sure it was legit. As it was, nobody did."

Keeping her focus on the crash, Gwen questioned, "The, um, body was gone by the time search and rescue found the crash site?"

His eyebrows rose. "Agent Bruce Kimball's body?"

That man she'd shot and killed. "Yes."

"No sign of it. No backboard. No proof anyone but the pilot was on board. To the contrary. The surroundings had been completely cleaned up. From what I know secondhand, it was assumed the pilot had deviated from his flight plan for an unknown reason, had a medical crisis or got caught in some weather anomaly and went down before he could let anyone know he was in trouble."

"I think Kimball must have killed him. Did Rafe tell you that?"

Rafe laid a hand on her shoulder. "I did. I told him everything that happened and all our speculation." He lifted his gaze to Zabrowsky. "What do you think?"

The already deep furrows in Ron Zabrowsky's forehead became chasms. "About the idea of staying with Ms. Allen."

Rafe's fingers tightened on Gwen's shoulder. "Yeah."

She held her breath.

"I have reservations for obvious reasons, but… it might work as a very temporary measure. Discovering we had an internal betrayal—" He broke off.

She didn't ask herself whether this was a good idea or whether she was just setting herself up for real heartbreak. She only knew she wanted this. Days if not weeks more with Rafe. Time to talk when they weren't running for their lives.

If it became awkward, if they turned out to have nothing in common, then that might be just as well.

"Gwen." Rafe crouched in front of her wheelchair, his hands covering hers where they rested on the arms. His dark eyes were searching. "Are you sure?"

"Of course I'm sure." To her ears, she sounded a little shaky. She hoped he hadn't noticed.

He kept looking into her eyes for an unnerving length of time before he gave her hands a quick squeeze and rose to his feet.

"Ron?"

"It would solve some immediate problems. You can't go with her right away, though. We need her to be seen making her way home alone." Zabrowsky gave her an apologetic glance. "Not that it's likely anyone is watching, but we can't afford to be careless."

Rafe's jaw had tightened, but Gwen nodded. "No. That makes sense."

"Then let's plan how we can slip him in late tonight."

Her chest expanded as if with the first full breath she'd been able to take in longer than she could remember. This wasn't goodbye—not yet.

Chapter Fifteen

"The pull-out sofa is fine," Rafe said even though what he'd really like was to sleep with her in the queen-size bed he'd caught a glimpse of in the single bedroom during the brief tour she'd given him after his 2:00 a.m. arrival. "You must be beat."

"I slept for a few hours." A smile lit her face. "*After* the best shower I've ever taken. I'm bitter the hospital personnel didn't let me shower then and there. They know me! But no—they sent me home in *filthy* clothes with *gross* hair. I won't be surprised if someone didn't take a few photos to post or at least pass around. Or maybe to blackmail me with."

He'd have been outraged if he hadn't been able to tell she was kidding. Who'd dislike the courageous, kind, patient woman who'd saved his life repeatedly?

And damn. Not even her visible bruises could keep him from thinking about how beautiful she was.

To distract himself, he said, "Ah, I didn't think to ask whether you have friends, neighbors, whatever, who are used to dropping by."

Her surprise was evident. "Not really. I'm not big on parties, and this place isn't large enough for me to host one, anyway. Usually, I meet friends out somewhere. With my work schedule being so different, even my closest friends can't keep track. When people call, I'll meet them somewhere else, like your boss suggested. That's usual for me, anyway. No one will wonder."

"Good." He dropped the duffel bag in a corner of the small living room. He unzipped it and removed the small toiletry kit, a result of the quick shopping trip Zabrowsky had personally made this evening while leaving Rafe stashed in that windowless, locked room in the hospital basement. It was unsettling that Zabrowsky was so determined to keep Rafe's reappearance among the living a deep, dark secret. He didn't dare even trust an underling enough to send him on the errand. The pilot and copilot of the helicopter that picked him and Gwen up were under orders to keep their damn mouths shut. The quote was straight from Zabrowsky. Rafe knew from experience that consequences for an indiscretion would be extreme.

At the moment, Gwen looked as uncomfortable as he felt. Him moving in with her here didn't feel like an extension of their desperate trek through the wilds of the park. It wasn't that he'd never had a roommate. During undercover investigations, he'd slept plenty of times in close quarters with the men he had to fit in with. In his personal life, it had been years. Generally when he was involved with a woman, overnights weren't included. He liked his space and privacy.

Had liked them, until he'd discovered the pleasure of holding this woman, waking to find her wrapped around him.

That's what he wanted right now and wasn't going to get.

"You probably haven't had any sleep yet at all, have you?" she said quickly. "I'll get out of your way. If you're up before me in the morning, I've programmed the coffee maker. Otherwise, help yourself to anything you can find. There isn't much, but I'll put in a grocery order in the morning. You can add to the list."

"Thanks."

"Well, then…" She backed up, bumped into the edge of the kitchen island and forced a smile. "Good night."

He opened his mouth, but she'd retreated down the extremely short hall to her bathroom, leaving him alone. For all that he was beat, he wasn't so sure sleep would come easily tonight.

HE'D BEEN RIGHT. The pull-out mattress was fine, if nowhere near as comfortable as his bed in his apartment had been, or the one at the safe house, for that matter. It was incomparable luxury compared to the thin, too narrow foam pad he and Gwen had shared the past few nights, so he couldn't use it to excuse his restlessness.

He did drop off, wake up and sleep again. The third time he came awake, he saw a faint glow coming from the bedroom or bathroom. Rafe lay still and waited. The toilet didn't flush; the light didn't go out. Finally, he climbed out of bed and walked on silent feet toward the source of the light: a six-inch crack where she'd left her bedroom door open.

He glanced down at himself and decided he was decent enough in pajama pants and a T-shirt from a package of three that had been part of his new wardrobe. He wrapped lightly on the door with his knuckles.

A no-doubt startled silence was followed by, "Rafe? Come in."

He pushed open the door and stepped into her bedroom. Gwen sat up in bed, pillows piled behind her, a laptop on crossed legs beneath the covers. Gleaming strands of golden-brown hair had worked their way loose from her braid.

"I'm sorry. Did I wake you up?" she asked.

He shook his head and wandered closer. "Wasn't sleeping well."

"The sofa—"

"Is fine. Just...have a lot on my mind." *Especially you*, he didn't say.

She smiled weakly. "Me too. I guess I shouldn't have slept earlier. Um... I was reading what coverage appeared in the *Seattle Times* about the crash."

"Yeah, I did that earlier. It's scanty, and what's there has no resemblance to what really happened."

"No." She looked shy. "If you want to sit down..."

On the bed, she meant. There were no other options. A dresser, bedside stand and treadmill filled most available floor space. He sat near the foot.

"You having nightmares?" he asked.

"I...don't really know." The uncertainty looked genuine. "I keep jerking awake, so my dreams probably aren't all sunshine and roses." Her forehead creased as she studied him. "What about you? Or... I suppose you become inured."

"To some extent." He talked for a minute about the necessity of being able to separate the ugly things he saw and did on the job from the rest of his life. He didn't mention that the process wasn't nearly as tidy as it sounded. "Right now, I'm having trouble remembering what the rest of my life was like," he heard himself say.

Where did that come from?

Her eyes were warm. "You were undercover for a year, you said. That's…a long time."

He moved his shoulders uncomfortably. Talking about feelings, that was something he did even less often than he went home, which he no longer had. He'd stored his possessions before taking on the last investigation.

"Then over a month in the safe house," he reminded her.

She closed her laptop and set it aside without looking away from him. "You must have friends."

"Sure." Rafe grimaced. Did he? Given that his best friend from growing up was dead, the closest to longtime friends he had were from college, and they were spread across the country and contact consisted mostly of an occasional phone conversation. "In my job, friends come and go. We get transferred, disappear for varying lengths of time. We intend to stay in touch but rarely do. It's hard to make friends outside the agency when you can't talk about most of what you do."

"No, I suppose not." She kept studying him. "What do you do for, well, recreation?"

"I run, lift weights, play in baseball and basketball leagues our agency fields. Join a regular poker group, read, watch TV." He shrugged. "On my rare vacations, I enjoy diving."

Gwen wrinkled her nose. "Diving in the Puget Sound isn't the same experience as it would be in the Caribbean."

He laughed. "So I hear. You've tried it, then?"

"Yes. I wasn't enthused. I did snorkel once in Hawaii and loved that."

He interpreted that as her saying she'd be open to diving again in warm, clear waters in some imaginary future with him.

They kept talking, voices low, sharing bits and pieces of their lives from the trivial to the important. Given the nighttime quiet, the atmosphere felt intimate. Just the two of them. They'd had that a lot recently, but this was different. He couldn't quite put his finger on why.

"What time is it?" he asked at last.

"Hm? Oh." She reached for her phone, which was plugged in on the bedside stand. "Five thirty. You should go back to sleep."

"I was thinking a cup of coffee sounds good. I'll try to be quiet—"

Gwen shook her head. "I would have gotten up earlier if I hadn't been trying not to wake you. I'll probably need a nap later, but hey! I don't have anything better to do."

With a yawn, he stretched his arms over his head, aware of a pull in the injured arm but overall appreciating more mobility than he'd have expected so soon. "You're able to go out, at least." Zabrowsky wanted anybody watching to see her follow a normal routine on days when she wasn't working. "Now, me, I'm free to do nothing but lounge on the couch and stare mindlessly at the TV."

"You don't even have a laptop, do you?"

A fact that irritated him no end. "Nope. And I won't have one."

"Well, you're welcome to use mine. And... surely you were given a phone."

"I was, but Ron made it clear he didn't want me online to do more than read news updates."

"Oh. Well, um, I do have the treadmill."

Rafe laughed. "And I'll use it, but probably not for a few more days."

She scrunched her face up. "Me either. So... I think there are some waffles in the freezer."

Accepting the signal, he stood. "I'd better get dressed."

It was while getting dressed in the bathroom, anticipating more than he should the very kind of breakfast he often had when hurried, that Rafe had an epiphany. That conversation really had been different. Simple as that. He'd never let himself talk to anyone as he had to Gwen. The closest might have been when he started a relationship with a girl in college, but it wouldn't have even crossed his mind to tell her about Mateo, as an example.

No, he and Gwen had shared like two people who really wanted to know each other, from the fun parts to the deep, hurtful places. They weren't on the run anymore; they were in the comfort of her home. What they'd gone through with each other had answered many of the biggest questions, meaning he could be open in a way he had never been with a woman.

The very fact that he really did want to know about everything that had made Gwen Allen the woman she was, from the heartbreaking to the trivial, shook him to his foundation. There was no question that he'd be walking out of her life soon. He knew better than to fall for her, if that's what was happening.

He stared at himself in the mirror. *Hell.* Maybe it was too late.

GWYN'S EMPLOYERS WEREN'T thrilled to have to remove her from the roster for a minimum of a month. After Zabrowsky confirmed in some mysterious way that nobody beyond the dispatcher at EMS Flight had had the slightest idea she'd gotten on that helicopter—and the dispatcher had been exceedingly grateful to be ordered to forget that he knew anything about it—she'd required a new excuse for her disappearance and injuries.

Apparently, federal agents were encouraged to be creative. Now she and an unnamed friend had gone backpacking without taking sensible precautions, like charging their phones. They'd gotten lost, after which Gwen stumbled over a cliff. The friend had helped her hobble out of the wilderness. Gwen made herself grovel while clenching her teeth and being officially reprimanded. She didn't appreciate any of it. The only plus side was that she didn't have to explain helping herself to narcotics or what she'd done with the missing doses.

Rafe's annoyance that her courageous conduct had been rewarded so shabbily helped her get over being mad. She even resented the implication that she and an apparently brainless friend would have been so careless as to forget to pack a charger for their phones.

He'd wrapped an arm around her while she grumbled.

"I don't blame you for being irritated," he said sympathetically, "but the story doesn't hang together if you'd carried a charger. Claiming no cell service might make someone wonder if you hadn't been in Mount Rainier National Park, and that's the last thing we want."

"Yeah, yeah." She sighed, letting herself lean into him for a moment, but not too long. The heat she occasionally saw in his eyes let her know that surrendering to temptation could have long-term consequences she was trying to avoid.

Like making love with a man she'd never be able to forget and might forever use as a standard other men couldn't match.

In the next couple of days, she learned he was a good roommate in most respects. He never complained about the confinement, although she felt his tension as if he exuded an electrical charge. He tried to work it out doing exercises— she was awestruck by the number of sit-ups he could do—and he hadn't been kidding about using the treadmill. He ran what had to be ten miles or more a day on it. They'd be talking in the kitchen, and he'd suddenly jump up and say, "I need a run," and vanish to her bedroom.

Which meant, of course, that she couldn't go to her bedroom, because then she'd have to feast on the sight of him in low-slung sweatpants and a tank top that exposed an imposing amount of muscle as he ran. Fast and hard until sweat dripped, until the intensity on his face almost frightened her.

He did that *right next to her bed*.

She couldn't help thinking of another excellent way for him to burn off some of that stress. She wanted to burn off her own that way, too, except for this fear that making love with him would be *too* good.

By the third day, she felt better enough to start going out occasionally, even though she felt guilty because Rafe was one hundred percent confined. Since she'd been assigned the task of appearing as if she were back from her vacation a little battered but otherwise normal, except for the frustration of not being able to work, she had to show her face. She met friends from work for coffee, stopped by base to say hi and listened to them talk with shock about the crash and the pilot's death.

"I mean, I've never flown with him," a trauma nurse who was a frequent partner of Gwen's said, "but..."

She didn't have to finish. The dead man could have been any of the pilots they knew well and appreciated with every flight. *They* could be on the next flight that went down, claiming all lives aboard.

Of course, Gwen couldn't admit that she'd met Bill, never mind seen his charred remains. Puked after seeing that. Shot and killed the man who'd been responsible.

She claimed headaches to avoid getting together with coworkers after that. Instead, she grocery-shopped and stopped at the pharmacy to keep up on birth control she hadn't needed in a very long time and didn't need right now, either, but it still seemed…smart. She bought a pair of expensive athletic shoes to replace the ones now tattered and stinky after the use she'd put them through. She picked up a newspaper daily at the box on the corner. Both she and Rafe read it voraciously.

And every time she left her apartment, she had the uncomfortable feeling that she was being watched. She never saw anyone seeming to pay attention to her, but she tried.

On the fifth day, Rafe received a phone call.

"Bodies?" he repeated, glanced at her and went to her bedroom. She heard the door close as she continued with dinner preparations.

When he reappeared, his expression was grim. "Zabrowsky says they found the bodies of the two men we shot." His jaw tightened.

Gwen guessed those bodies weren't in good shape by this time.

"They also found a SAT radio that might have flown out of a pocket when one of them went down. It was deep in some ferns and other underbrush."

Her hands, one holding a paring knife, stopped,

unmoving, above the cutting board and a half-chopped bell pepper. "A radio."

"That means they probably did report on us when they saw us descending the ridge. They know a woman was with me, likely even gave a description of you."

Her breathing had become choppy, and she looked down to see that her hands trembled. Carefully, she set down the knife. "They still don't know my name," she pointed out.

"It gets worse," Rafe continued. "The dispatcher who okayed you on that flight admits now to a phone call that came in three or four days after the helicopter went down. Somebody claiming to be a cousin wanted to be sure a woman made it onto a flight that was supposed to be going directly to Seattle. Since you hadn't been in touch, the caller claimed to be worried. He evidently confirmed you boarded the helicopter but can't remember whether he used your name when he agreed."

"Oh, God. You're not safe here. You need to leave."

"If they'd found you, we'd know."

"What?" She stared at him. "Somebody could be watching me."

"Somebody is."

"You're kidding."

"Why would I kid?" He sounded genuinely bewildered.

"Because I've had this creepy feeling that I'm being watched!" she cried. "I told myself I was imagining things, that it was just a leftover from when we knew we *were* being hunted, but now you're telling me…?" Conflicted emotions choked off everything else she wanted to say.

"I'm sorry." Rafe came to her, turned her slowly and pulled her against him, his arms wrapping her snugly. "I should have said something. With this kind of informal arrangement, Ron just about had to keep an eye on us. He and I agreed on a female agent we've both worked with before and believe in. Figured a woman would be less conspicuous."

Dark-haired, medium-height, friendly smile. Gwen had seen the same woman several times and just assumed she was new in the neighborhood. When she described her, Rafe nodded. "That's Carolyn."

Gwen debated between shoving him away and continuing to lean on his strong body. Outrage versus the usual temptation, which won. She punched him in the shoulder, anyway. The uninjured one, of course.

Finally, head resting on his shoulder, she said, "You're confident she'll spot anyone else following me or lurking around the building."

"That's the idea."

The answer wasn't as complete as she'd have liked, but how could he give her a guarantee? She'd agreed to a level of risk when she offered him sanctuary with her. *Live with it*, she told herself.

"Okay," she mumbled.

Being held might have been comfortable if she hadn't been so aware that they were in full body contact—her thighs and breasts pressed against his chest, her cheek on her shoulder. And, was he getting aroused? He didn't say anything, just stayed exceptionally still.

Gwen realized she was doing the same.

Abruptly, his arms dropped from around her, and he backed away. "If you don't need help with dinner, I'm going to use the treadmill."

"This is getting to you, isn't it?"

"This?" he echoed sharply.

"I mean—" Gwen gestured "—being trapped in such a small space. It must feel like a prison cell."

A rough sound escaped him. "It's not the space. You have to know that."

The hot light in his dark eyes transfixed her. "I…wondered," she whispered. "You…get to me, too, you know."

"I swore I'd keep my hands off you."

She knew suddenly how much better having

even a single memory of a night with him would be than nothing.

Warmth flushed her cheeks and she swallowed. "I wish you wouldn't."

One long stride, and his mouth closed over hers.

As if they'd done this a thousand times, they kissed deeply, intensely, tongues stroking and tangling. He gripped her butt to lift her higher while his other hand cupped her jaw. Gwen quit thinking, quit worrying and only felt. She slung her arm around his neck and rose on tiptoe. She wanted to touch him everywhere, but right now, the best she could do was to slide her free hand under his T-shirt and stroke the hard muscles in his back while her fingertips traced his vertebrae.

She wanted everything.

He nipped her lower lip and raised his head. "Gwen?" he asked hoarsely. "Are you sure?"

She wouldn't have sworn she could talk at all, but she managed. "I'm sure."

He said something gritty she couldn't make out, swept her high in his arms and carried her out of the kitchen and toward the bed where she'd felt so alone since he came home with her.

Chapter Sixteen

His hands were shaking. He'd never wanted a woman as much as he did this one, and it had been scaring the hell out of him. He'd have no choice but to leave her. Right now, though, he could give her everything he could.

Instead of throwing her down on the bed, he let her slide down his body until she was back on her feet. The friction with her curves felt so damn good, he wanted to do it again. Instead, he looked down at her face, so vulnerable, her cheeks pink, her eyes dazed, dreamy. She wanted this, too. He eased her shirt over her head, careful not to hurt her, and unclipped her bra, letting it fall. Then he stared, drinking in the sight of her long, pale torso and high, full breasts with delectable rosy nipples.

"I have to—" He lifted her again so he could lick and kiss and suck one of her breasts, then the other.

She whimpered and said something he thought might be "Not fair."

He did most of the stripping, but she helped. He was just trying to decide how he could bend over far enough with this erection to untie his shoes when she knelt at his feet. Rafe watched helplessly as she tugged off first one, then the other and finally his socks. Still on her knees, she squeezed his calves with strong hands before trailing them over his thighs and higher, until his back bowed in a combination of ecstasy and agony that forced him to take control again.

Once he had her on her back in bed, he stroked and tasted and kissed her until he was shaking again. Her legs spread, her knees tightened on his hips, and he had a horrifying realization. For the first time in his life, he wasn't sure he could stop, but he had to.

He pulled back. "I don't have a condom."

"I bought some a few days ago. Just in case. But I'm on birth control, anyway."

He had never dared trust a woman to that extent. This time…he did. Gwen wouldn't lie, but no one method of birth control was entirely safe, and he wouldn't be around. He couldn't take a chance.

"Where are they?"

"Drawer."

He fumbled, tore open a box with one hand,

ripped the small packet even faster and covered himself.

And then he buried himself inside her, never taking his eyes from hers.

She moved with him as if she knew what he needed—or as if she needed the same. With one keening cry, she came with shocking speed, tightening around him until he groaned out her name and spilled himself inside her. If he hadn't been wearing the condom— *Don't think it.*

Rafe came down heavily on her, barely able to make himself move and roll to one side. She rolled with him, her head finding the familiar resting place, their bodies fitting together as if they were one.

Both sated and stunned, Rafe wished he could absorb her. He'd be happy to stay just like that for the rest of his life.

And if anything had ever rattled him, it was that thought.

NEITHER SAID A word in the aftermath. They did finally have dinner, avoiding even a glance at the elephant in the room. Gwen worried aloud about the earlier phone call. Rafe reassured her when he didn't believe himself.

If those bastards had her name or had even learned she was a paramedic with EMS Flight who'd hitched a ride on the helicopter that carried him, they'd find her. She was right—he should insist that he be moved *now*, except that would leave her alone. Here, he had a chance of protecting her. How would he feel if he'd been settled in another damn rambler in Idaho or Minnesota or South Carolina only to be told Gwen was dead?

That…really wasn't a question. Rafe didn't think he could live with the knowledge she'd died for him. He had a bad feeling he was head over heels in love with her, although it was hard to be sure since he'd never experienced anything like this before.

He cleaned up after dinner while keeping an eye on her. She plopped down on the couch and turned on the TV, going to local news on a Seattle channel. Rafe didn't know if she'd always been a news junkie, but she certainly qualified now. What did she think the air-brushed newscasters could tell her that she didn't already know…or fear?

When he joined her, sinking down on the cushion right next to hers and laying his arm around her shoulders, she didn't even look at him. He hoped it was his imagination that she stiffened. Whatever topic the reporters currently covered had them laughing. He didn't pay any attention.

"Are you sorry?" he asked abruptly.

Gwen turned sharply to scrutinize him. "You mean, about…? Of course I'm not! I've been… attracted to you since you were still strapped down and I was told you were a criminal."

"Ah." He relaxed. "I thought you were beautiful from the minute you uncovered my eyes, too. An angel of mercy, despite the fact that I was desperate to see where I was."

She made a face at the humor in his voice. "I did a lot more important things for you than that."

Even that flicker of amusement left him. "Yeah, you did. You'll have nightmares about them for years."

"No. I didn't do anything that wasn't necessary. And I'm not like most people, you know. I see terrible things on the job. We might pick up an injured person from a five-car pileup on the freeway, but we also see all the people, adults and children who didn't survive long enough even to have a chance."

Rafe knew that but had let himself forget. He'd say her job was what made her tougher than average, quicker thinking, willing to face danger most people would shrink from—except that her determination to become a paramedic said something about who she'd been all along. If she had nightmares, they were probably still about being trapped in that car as a child with her mother's body inches away.

He drew her to him and kissed her, maybe roughly, he didn't know, just that he had to have her again right now. With a sound that was nearly a sob, Gwen flung herself at him and kissed him back with all the passion he felt. At one point, he became irritated enough at the canned voices coming from the TV to stab a button on the remote and shut the damn thing up. That was the closest to a conscious thought he had.

Otherwise, he struggled to get her clothes off and enough of his so that he could make love to her again. The bedroom was too far away. He laid her back on the couch, pushed into her and kept thrusting until her climax flung him into his own.

Then he got the rest of his clothes off and did it again.

It wasn't until an hour later, as she led him by one hand to bed, that he remembered he hadn't used a condom either time. Despite knowing she was on birth control, his carelessness would have panicked him normally. This time, he had a tantalizing vision of her swelling with his baby.

He made sure she couldn't see his face while he shut down a dream he couldn't allow himself. What he felt for her was too new. Those emotions were the equivalent of tiny green shoots emerging from the soil. Most new growth ended up frozen because of late cold snaps or fried in a midsummer drought or trampled under uncaring feet.

Rafe couldn't let himself forget that he wouldn't be around this fall or next spring or probably even next fall. Imagining that whatever he felt for Gwen, or her for him, would survive a year and a half absence was too much of a stretch to be believable.

The kindest thing he could do would be to make it clear to her that this thing between them wasn't going anywhere. Because it wasn't.

But he might have a few more days, a few more nights, and he couldn't make himself hurt her now—or miss the chance to have mind-blowing sex as often as possible.

Call him selfish, but he'd never lied to Gwen. She knew as well as he did that they were existing in a tiny slice of time that could be snatched away from them any minute.

For all the passion she showed him, she didn't ask for reassurance that he cared about her. Even as that was a relief, it bothered him. They made love twice more that night but never discussed it.

He remembered her saying something about

going out for a few casual errands the next day, but wrinkled her nose when he asked her plans and said, "Maybe tomorrow. Unless there's something you need, I'm happy here." Her smile teased and tempted. "It's not like we're bored."

"No." He hadn't been bored a minute since he'd set eyes on her. There'd been days when he'd felt like a big cat pacing the perimeter of his cage in search of a weakness, but boredom hadn't been the reason for that. Nope. It was all about Gwen.

Right now, all he wanted was to extend the days with her as long as possible.

Ron called that evening. "I can't find any hint that Bruce Kimball wasn't working alone, at least out of the Chicago office. I spoke to his supervising special agent, who admitted there have been some issues with him. Mostly personality clashes, attitude. He was close to being terminated. Knowing that might have motivated him to take a big paycheck, although you'd think he'd have been smart enough to know the odds weren't good a cartel would let him live once he'd served his purpose."

"No."

"Given what I've learned—and what I haven't learned—I'm going to have you moved to a new safe house. Expect to hear from me in the next day or two."

"Will do."

Ron ended the call. Feeling almost numb, Rafe sat on the edge of Gwen's bed. Tell her how soon he was going? Or wait until he had no choice?

His conscience twinging, all he could think was *Hell*.

SOMETHING CHANGED AFTER the phone call Rafe took in her bedroom that evening. When Gwen asked about it, he only shook his head, his expression impassive in that way he had when he was in special agent mode.

She couldn't help immediately speculating. Had he learned that other agents had been compromised, too, and was sick with disappointment or anger? Had the Espinosa family shifted practices or personnel in a way that would make Rafe's testimony less powerful to a jury? Or had the call been from someone else altogether, perhaps giving him personal news?

The reminder was timely. Despite their closeness, she didn't know much about his personal life. He enjoyed playing poker and baseball. His parents, he'd talked about. What happened with his friend Mateo, which she thought he'd offered up because she'd told him about the car accident that had killed her mother and changed the trajectory of Gwen's life. Otherwise, surely

a man who looked like Rafe and had his cha-
risma and wicked smile usually had a girlfriend.
Probably not a live-in one currently, not after
his year plus spent undercover, but there could
still be someone for whom he cared deeply.

Gwen rolled her eyes. Way to feel sorry for
herself. He kept warning her in his not-so-sub-
tle way that what they enjoyed was temporary.
In other words, he wasn't until-death-do-us-
part in love with *her*.

Too bad she did love him. Her little secret.

The next morning, she asked if he needed
anything when she went out.

Sitting at the table with a cup of coffee in
front of him, he frowned. "Nothing I can't live
without."

"To rephrase, is there anything you *want*?"

His grin came close to making her knees
buckle, except…it didn't seem to reach his
eyes. Disturbed, she still didn't protest when
he tugged her forward, slipped a hand behind
her neck and urged her to bend over enough for
him to kiss her.

"You," he whispered. "I want you."

But apparently didn't need her.

She emerged from the kiss, smiled at him and
said, "I may buy all kinds of goodies while I'm
out. You'll be sorry."

"I'll live with it."

Gwen grabbed her handbag, dropped her phone in it, made sure she had her keys and said, "Bye."

Too bad there was nowhere she especially wanted to go or anyone she needed to see.

Behave normally, she'd been ordered. Now that the bruises on her face had faded from sight and the lump on her head was gone, her only remaining physical symptom was soreness from her bruised rib cage. Give her another week, and she'd probably be able to persuade a doctor to clear her to go back to work.

What then?

Rafe would be gone. She knew that with painful certainty, one she both forced herself to confront and pushed back at. Why torture herself?

She let herself out of the apartment, took the elevator down and strolled out. She hadn't gone a block when she caught a glimpse of an attractive dark-haired woman sitting at a bus stop apparently intent on her phone. Carolyn.

Carolyn didn't so much as glance toward Gwen, who ignored her, too. As far as she could tell, the agent didn't follow her, or if she did, she had a gift for subterfuge.

Gwen went to her favorite neighborhood grocery store, not huge and really expensive because of the superior quality of their produce and breads. This was the only place she ever bought cherry tomatoes because they'd be really ripe and tasty. Maybe she'd make a favorite recipe tonight with cherry tomatoes and dumplings.

She browsed, bought more than she needed and had enough to carry after she checked out to give her an excuse to skip any other errands.

Half a block from her building, just passing an alley, she saw something strange. A foot stuck out from behind a dumpster. Probably one of the houseless people who called this neighborhood home, she thought, although this was the middle of the day. And…the athletic shoe on the foot was bright white with a logo she recognized. Those shoes weren't cheap.

Carolyn had been wearing those shoes.

Gwen's step stalled. She should check, be sure it wasn't Carolyn or anyone else who needed help. But the leap of her pulse said, *You can't help.* She had to pretend not to notice, keep an eye around herself and hurry home while trying very hard not to *look* as if she were hurrying.

And…call Rafe?

She started to fumble in her bag, but she'd be home in a matter of minutes. In fact, the steps into the building were just ahead. She bounded up them, smiled vaguely at another tenant who had been coming out and held the door for her, and stole a look back the direction she'd come.

Two men had their gazes on her and were walking fast.

Gwen dashed in, pushed the button for the elevator and leaped in when it proved to be on the ground floor. The doors shut, giving her a momentary illusion of safety, but the elevator seemed to take forever to rise to her floor.

Once she was in her apartment, she and Rafe could hold anyone off, couldn't they? She should have called to warn him—maybe she still should?—but the elevator glided to a stop and the doors parted.

She ran and was fumbling to get her key in the lock when she heard the metal door at the head of the staircase slam open not twenty feet from her. Running footsteps thudded toward her as the apartment door gave way, and she screamed, "Rafe!"

HE FELT RESTLESS, but not in a way running mindlessly on the treadmill would help. In fact, had he stepped foot on it since the first time he and Gwen had made love?

He shook his head hard. He never liked it when Gwen went out by herself, for all practical purposes setting herself up as bait, although she didn't seem to realize that was what Ron had in mind.

Part of what Ron had in mind, anyway.

Today his uneasiness grew even though she hadn't been gone all that long. Nothing like when she'd met friends for coffee. For all he knew, she'd taken the bus to the university bookstore to browse and would be gone for a couple of hours. She hadn't said.

But half an hour after she went out the door, he began to pace. Every so often, he'd crack the blinds at the front of the small living room to let him see the street and some of the sidewalk. He'd try to make himself sit but was too antsy to be still for long, and the next thing he knew, he'd be up and walking again.

Ten feet that way, twenty-five if he went through the kitchen and down the very short hall, too. Then back. Peek through the blinds. Repeat.

Instead of leaving his gun sitting on an end table, he slipped it in his waistband at the back for quick access. Did Gwen carry Kimball's, which Ron had not asked her to return? Rafe realized he didn't know. Maybe just as well if it wasn't deep in that capacious handbag of hers. She'd proven herself a good shot, but even the best of police marksmen didn't dare open fire on a busy sidewalk with passing cars and buses. She didn't have their experience.

This time when he scanned the sidewalk, he saw two men walking fast in this direction. Nothing that would catch most people's attention—they could be hurrying to catch a bus or late getting back to their desks at work—but he didn't like the look of them. The thermometer was supposed to top ninety degrees today, hot by northwestern standards, but one wore a jacket and the other a denim overshirt.

He didn't see Gwen, but he'd swear their speed increased. Then they moved out of sight—as if they'd turned into this or a neighboring building.

He heard the elevator and tensed. Let it be Gwen. Feet that had to be running in the hall. Rafe had just reached the door when it opened and Gwen threw herself forward, yelling, "Rafe!"

Seconds later, a man brandishing a handgun shoved her in.

Rafe pulled his gun even as a bullet splintered the glass on a piece of framed art on the wall. He immediately noted from the thickness of their upper bodies that they wore Kevlar vests.

Gwen screamed and staggered, the second man having gripped her ponytail and using it to whip her to one side.

Rafe dove behind the easy chair as a bullet burned his arm. From behind the minimal cover, he fired without his usual icy calm. He wouldn't take a chance of hitting Gwen, but if he didn't take these two down, both he and Gwen would die.

The chair jumped from a fusillade of bullets. Only a decade and a half of practice and experience allowed him to aim carefully instead of firing wildly. He didn't like headshots, but throats…

The first attacker went down, gun skittering across the floor toward Rafe. The second man, a brawny blue-eyed blond, wrenched Gwen in front of him, her head pulled painfully back, and pressed the barrel of his handgun at her temple.

"Drop the gun! I'll kill her! You know I will."

Rafe calculated. If he dropped his Glock, would he have time to get his hands on the other gun that lay temptingly close to him? Would the piece of scum turn his sights on Rafe the minute he moved or shoot Gwen and throw her aside as if she were a distraction done serving his purpose?

"I'll put it down," he called. "Let her go."

The creep laughed. Gwen made a gurgling sound.

Rafe gathered himself, laid his Glock on the

floor and gently pushed it away. At the very moment he launched himself forward for the other weapon, the man holding Gwen started swinging his gun toward Rafe.

Chapter Seventeen

Gwen grabbed her assailant's arm and shoved it up.

Bullets flew over Rafe's nearly supine body. He snatched up the gun he'd gone for, raised it and risked a couple of shots at the arm and shoulder, away from Gwen.

Her captor reeled and kept shooting wildly as he went down, bringing Gwen with him. Rafe leaped forward to free her from the grip on her hair, except she hammered a fist down on the fool's wounded arm. He screamed, letting go of both her ponytail and his gun. Rafe took barely five seconds to flip him face down on the blood-slick oak floor.

"Call 911!" he ordered, drilling his knee into the man's back. "Check the other guy."

She sensibly did that first. "He's dead," she said, almost calmly, and a moment later, he heard her talking to a dispatcher.

Zabrowsky would not be happy about this

debacle, except his witness was alive, and there wouldn't have to be an explanation as to why an innocent local woman had been killed.

Rafe felt sick at how close it had been.

Gwen turned as she ended the call and said, "I have to go down and let them in."

"You're not hurt?" he asked hoarsely.

She was shaking but shook her head. "You are. You're bleeding."

"Nothing significant." How had he sounded so calm? After surveying her, he said, "You have blood on you, too. You have time to change shirts."

Without a word, she turned and disappeared into her bedroom. She returned looking almost pristine, except for the shock and stress on her face and a ponytail that was wildly askew.

Rafe had rarely felt a desire to kill unnecessarily, but right this minute, the relentless effort to hunt him and Gwen down, the ruthlessness of it, weighed on his shoulders, and he stared down at the profile of the first of their attackers, who'd survived.

"Nobody would know if I broke your neck," he said, almost conversationally.

The bastard was smart enough not to beg for mercy. Not that he'd be getting any. He would undoubtedly go away for a good long while.

"You're not worth it," Rafe said decidedly.

Within minutes, the apartment was overrun by emergency personnel. A medic treated Rafe, determining the bullet was a through and through, and although she bandaged his arm, she encouraged him to have a doctor look at it, too.

With a sense of unreality, he looked around. He'd seen dozens of similar scenes. No, that was an understatement. Bullet holes decorated the walls and had torn the chair Gwen most often sat in to shreds and broken pieces of wood. Everyone stepped around the broken glass from the framed art that now hung drunkenly on the wall. The contents in grocery bags she must have dropped were smashed flat. Something red leaked from one of them. He glanced up; yeah, there were even a few bullet holes in the ceiling. Thank God this was the top floor of the apartment building.

She stood in the kitchen out of the way, pressed to the lower cabinets, her expression stricken. Did she have insurance that would cover this mess? How would the landlord react? Would she be able to give an explanation resembling anything close to the real story about what happened?

No, of course not. Zabrowsky would work his wizardry, expect silence from the responding cops, and Gwen would be stuck as the victim of a vicious home invasion assault.

And Rafe? He was powerless and knew it.

First, the injured assailant was removed, and finally, after the appearance of a pair of detectives who asked questions Rafe and Gwen had already answered but did again, the body was zipped into a bag and also hauled away.

Sometime during the chaos, Rafe had disappeared long enough to make a phone call. She didn't like the expression on his face when he reappeared. She'd have called it desperation if she hadn't known better.

He wouldn't be allowed to stay here any longer; she did know that.

The door had no sooner shut behind the detectives, leaving her alone with Rafe, than he said, "Give me your bank account number. I'll make sure you're reimbursed, even if I have to do it myself."

As if they'd ever let him trot off to a bank or even access his own account from a safe house. But she nodded numbly, called up her own account on her phone and scribbled the numbers on a piece of paper that he pocketed.

"This is it, then?" she asked, holding on to her pride with both hands.

"I'm afraid so." He looked around. "You've paid a high price for getting sucked into my problems."

"I don't regret it." She didn't move. Her eyes might be burning, but she refused to let a tear fall until he was gone. "If somebody is coming soon, you'd better make sure you have everything together."

"Gwen…"

She tried to smile. "If you're going to tell me you're madly in love with me and will be back in a year or so—"

Of course, he was shaking his head before she got that far. "You know I can't say that. I won't forget you, but I'm looking at a minimum of a year, maybe as much as two years, before the trial is behind me. I might as well be going to prison in the meantime. You need to move on with your life. I can't promise anything."

That last sentence seemed to be torn from him, as if—No, she wouldn't delude herself.

"I'll be fine. Back to work before I know it."

To give herself something to do, she grabbed a black plastic bag from beneath the kitchen sink and started by sweeping up the glass. Rafe picked up shreds and broken pieces of her chair to add them to the bag.

They'd mostly straightened what was left in her small living room when a knock came on the door. Rafe looked through the peephole, a safety feature that was one of the reasons she'd rented this apartment—and had been so much help today—and let a man and woman in. If she'd seen them on the street, she'd have guessed they were FBI agents from their clothes and their sharply observant expressions. But nope, they were DEA instead. Apparently, feds all looked alike.

One kept an eye on Gwen as he asked Rafe, "You ready?"

"Yeah." He sounded hoarse, turned to face her.

She just shook her head. "We've said everything. You...take care, Rafe. Try to avoid any more bullet holes, okay?"

He almost smiled, then was gone.

Gwen locked the door behind them, and finally let herself collapse.

SHE DIDN'T GO back to EMS Flight. The higher-ups were jerks about her injury and need for weeks off, and then were shocked to hear she'd been the victim of a home invasion. Gwen didn't like the attitude and resigned. Medical helicopter rescue organizations all across the country were desperate for paramedics as well trained and experienced as she was. She wouldn't have any trouble finding a new job.

Once she did her best to repair her apartment and dealt with the landlord, she made the decision to move away from the area. Here, she caught glimpses of Rainier from city streets, and it dominated the skyline every time she went up in a helicopter. She loved Seattle and the Northwest, and she'd be leaving behind a lot of friends, but…she needed a change. To go someplace she wouldn't be constantly reminded of Rafe.

She tried to convince herself it wasn't him so much as the crash, followed by the traumatic days fleeing through incredibly rough country to escape armed pursuers—all culminating in the horrifying attack in her own apartment. But she knew better. It was all about him.

He hadn't even been in her life two full weeks, but she'd fallen in love with him. They'd… meshed, maybe in part because they'd both learned to guard themselves from the sight of desperate survivors of violence, accidental and otherwise. Of course, she arrived in the aftermath, while he might have been part of a whole bunch of shoot-outs, for all she knew. Or, worse, he'd had to see men or women tortured and been unable to do a thing to stop it because he'd been undercover and had to stay in the role if he was ever to bring down the monsters he investigated.

Maybe he wasn't capable of loving a woman, or maybe she just wasn't the right one; she didn't know. Only that she had to believe him when he told her to forget him and move on. Well, he hadn't said the "forget him" part, but he'd meant it.

She couldn't go back to her life as if nothing had happened. A complete change was what she needed.

Gwen applied for several jobs in parts of the country she thought she might like and finally accepted one with CALSTAR in Central California. She was able to live within visiting distance of San Francisco, a city with a flavor of its own that she quickly grew to love, but had a halfway affordable apartment in Stockton. She made friends, if not as close as the ones she'd left behind, had an alert on her phone for any news about the Espinosa family and read articles about the never-ending battle against drug trafficking in general, the profitability of fentanyl and connections to the Mexican cartels, and major DEA operations. Nothing ever popped up closely enough related to the operation Rafe had described, admittedly in skimpy detail, for her to believe it had to do with him.

Months later, when she let herself think about him, she imagined him trapped indoors all this time, able to do nothing but run on a treadmill, maybe lift weights, read, watch TV, chat with fellow agents who shuttled in and out to protect him. It had to be driving him mad. Of course, some of those agents were women—she thought about Carolyn, but nobody had ever told her whether Carolyn had lived or died—

so maybe he had a sexual partner. Or would he let himself, when the other agents who were around would know all about it?

Probably not.

She convinced herself it was good she didn't have a photo of him and couldn't find one online. Sooner or later, she'd forget what he looked like. Anyway, she'd mostly quit thinking about him, although the anniversary of him walking out of her life was hard. She was grateful that she had to work and that she was busy. Also that no one died that day, or she'd have had to feel guilty about being glad her services were needed.

I'll meet someone, she tried desperately to convince herself. She mixed with cops, firefighters, doctors and other emergency personnel. There had to be a man among them who'd measure up to Rafe Salazar and who would also be attracted to her. No, not just attracted—who would fall in love with her. Who wouldn't be able to sleep with her but then shrug and say, *Move on with your life.*

Except he'd also said, *I won't forget you.* And, *I can't promise you anything.* Both of which made her wonder if he had felt more for her than he'd admitted, if there was any chance at all—

Of course there wasn't.

The intercom blared to life, calling her unit to

Interstate 5 and a head-on collision with at least three fatalities and several critical survivors. Probably other helicopters would be needed, too.

RAFE HAD THOUGHT himself to be patient. Damn it, he'd *known* what he was getting into when he'd agreed to go deep undercover with one of the most notorious illegal drug manufacturing and trafficking organizations in North America. After the assault on the safe house and the death of two fellow agents—good guys—and then the ruthless disregard for Gwen's life as he was hunted, Rafe had been even more determined.

That was a year ago. A year during which he couldn't say he was actually living. *Existing* was a more accurate word. Updates on progress were rare. He got to wondering whether he'd been forgotten, whether warrants were being issued at all or whether no one wanted to admit to him that his testimony wouldn't be enough and he'd now thrown away *two years* of his life.

Except for the days—weeks—with Gwen. Those, he fixated on like a shipwrecked man might the broken piece of his boat that kept him afloat. It was downright pathetic.

He was stunned when things actually started to move, and he had to concentrate on reviewing material and reviving his memories of the hellish year he'd served as a useful underling while pretending to ignore assassinations taking place right in front of him and terrorization of whole towns where the cartel operated.

Turned out, getting excited didn't mean the first and biggest trial was actually starting. Arrests did finally take place, including a DEA operation that scooped up the head of the family who'd been in hiding, a man Rafe particularly despised. Rafe would be very glad to testify that he'd seen Papa Espinosa himself hold a gun to a Mexican police officer's temple and pull the trigger, after which he'd curled his lip and walked away while others hustled to toss the body into the back of an SUV and take it away.

Jury selection commenced and dragged on.

Fifteen months after he'd said goodbye to Gwen, Ron Zabrowsky brought him a couple of new suits and hustled him to a hotel in Houston, where he'd stay for the duration of the trial. It might drag on for weeks, and, yeah, there were at least two more in which his testimony would be required, but he saw the light at the end of the tunnel. And he knew that he'd come to the right decision for him.

The day the final trial ended, triumphantly or not, he was turning in his resignation.

GWEN WALKED AWAY from the helicopter carrying debris from their latest mission. Not the body— that waited for the morgue van. A sixty-four-year-old man had been nailed in a crosswalk by a speeding car that tossed him twenty feet or more to land on his head on the pavement. The driver didn't stop. An unusually observant teenager had noted at least part of the license plate number, which had the cops hopeful they'd be able to make an arrest in this particular hit-and-run. CALSTAR had been called because the incident had happened in a small town without a medical facility. An ambulance would have been too slow getting the victim to a trauma center.

But despite offering first-line trauma care themselves, he hadn't made it. From the moment she'd knelt at his side, she'd known he wouldn't live.

Thank God this was the end of her shift and she had a couple of days off coming to her. She felt as tired and discouraged as she had in a long time. A chill February wind tore hair from her braid and made her long for a hot shower.

"Call me shallow," her partner and friend who walked beside her said, "but that is one nice-looking man."

Gwen hardly noticed nice-looking men anymore, but she said, "Yeah? Where?" Her words dried up. That couldn't be—

The tall, dark and handsome man leaning against the door leading into their quarters straightened as he saw them approaching. Gwen quit walking. Didn't even notice that Nancy stopped, looked from one to the other and tactfully kept going.

"Rafe?" Gwen whispered.

He started toward her. "Yeah. It's me." He sounded as hoarse as he had when he said goodbye. "It's been a long time…"

"It has." She was surprised she could speak at all beyond his name. She didn't know what to feel.

"And I told you to forget me."

"No, that's one thing you didn't say. You said I should move on with my life." She gestured vaguely at the airfield and the bright red helicopter behind her. "I have."

"We hadn't known each other that long."

Her head bobbed.

He stopped right in front of her, head bent so he could look into her eyes with all the intensity she'd never forgotten. "If I'd said anything else, it wouldn't have been fair to you."

Wow. Suddenly, she wanted to scream at him. A year and a half of misery, and that was *fair*? But she also understood. His year and a half couldn't have been any better than hers, even if he hadn't been pining for her.

"I get it." Then she blinked, realizing. "The trial is over? Did you win?"

He grinned, doing impossible things to her heart. "Multiple trials. Once the head of the family was convicted of a dozen charges, including first-degree murder, his two sons, a cousin and five men who were also high-ranked went down like bowling pins."

"Then the entire cartel is done for?"

Now his smile twisted. "The leadership, but someone else will step into their place. And there are other cartels, other drug traffickers. It's a triumph, a warning to the rest of them, but we never achieve real victory in this fight."

"Oh, Rafe." Loaded down as she was with several bags, she could only reach out with one hand. "I'm sorry. Glad for you, too. I mean, you did more than anyone could have expected, but you sacrificed a lot for it, too."

He lifted one of the bags from her shoulder and gripped her hand. "I sacrificed any chance of a relationship with you."

She'd taken a step before what he said sunk in and she stopped again, swinging around to look at him. "That's what you were doing?"

"What would you call it?"

"I suppose I thought…"

"Thought?" he prodded, voice getting sharper.

Oh, just say it. "That you were just as glad to

have an excuse to leave without having some kind of big scene."

Now his eyebrows shot up. "You don't consider having your apartment shot up, the guy you were sleeping with shot and him getting hauled away by a couple of federal agents while leaving you holding the bag a *scene*?"

A laugh she'd never expected bubbled up in her. "Now that you mention it…"

He offered her a friendly grin that looked only slightly forced and said, "I'm told you're going off shift. Can we find someplace to talk?"

"Of course." She might as well be on a roller coaster, because suddenly tears blurred her vision. Despite the various bags and her being less than clean, she threw herself at him. "Oh, Rafe! I didn't think I'd ever see you again."

He pulled her close with his free arm. "God, Gwen. I missed you. If you're involved with someone, I understand, but—" He didn't finish, because she was sniveling against his shoulder.

She forced herself to lift her head. "I'm not. I…couldn't."

His dark eyes searched hers. "Even though you'd given up on me?"

"I guess I couldn't quite."

He bent and rested his forehead against hers, and for a moment, neither moved. Then he said gruffly, "Can we get out of here?"

Gwen wiped her tears on his denim shirt. "Absolutely."

Naturally, she took him home to an apartment that was barely bigger than the one she'd had in Seattle. He followed her in a shiny sedan she suspected was a rental, and was able to use a visitor slot in her parking garage.

The moment they got there, she begged off and took a quick shower. When she came out, he'd made coffee and offered her a cup.

Seeing something on her face, he said, "Bad day?"

"Until I saw you."

Sitting on a stool at the breakfast bar, he separated his legs and drew her to stand between them. "Tell me about it?"

Gwen did, seeing the understanding in his eyes. When she was done, she asked, "How long do you have? Zabrowsky doesn't have the nerve to call the time in a safe house a vacation, does he?"

Rafe laughed at that. "Even he's not that brazen." He hesitated. "After leaving the courthouse the last day, I quit my job. My schedule is entirely open."

Weirdly, she didn't feel the need to ask him why he'd done that. *Or maybe not so weirdly*, she thought, after what he'd said about the hopelessness of stopping the drug trafficking.

But he led her to the couch in her living room, and they sat as they had so many other times, her curled up next to him, and he talked. When he was done, he tipped his head so he could see her face.

"I guess I just have to ask." Without moving a muscle, he still appeared to be bracing himself. "Are you open to picking up where we left off in Seattle?"

She suddenly wasn't sure she could draw a breath. "That's what you want?"

"It's what I want." He hesitated, his expression becoming wary. "It happened fast, but I fell hard for you. I've never felt close to the same about any other woman."

Gwen wanted to burst into sobs, which was a completely counterintuitive response. After sucking in a breath—yes, she could still do it— she said, "Yes. Please. I fell for you, too. You had to have known."

He swallowed. "I hoped. *God.*" He pulled her onto his lap and kissed her. They didn't talk after that for a long while.

By the time they got dressed again and she called to order some Thai food to be delivered, she asked what he intended to do professionally and offered to move anywhere he could get a job.

"I can work anywhere," she said.

Rafe's smile crinkled the skin at the corners of his eyes. "I figured. I think I'll stay in law enforcement, but something local." He shrugged. "I could get on with San Francisco PD, but I think I'd like a smaller town."

It didn't take them long to agree that they'd take a good look around and do some serious thinking before they decided. And that in the meantime, taking up where they left off was exactly what they'd do. Only this time, fear had no claim over them.

The last thing she said on the verge of sleep was "I can't believe this."

As he pulled her into a wonderfully familiar embrace, he murmured in a low, deep voice, "I'm here for good."

* * * * *